Kidnapped by the Bratva

Forced Marriage Mafia Romance

Morozov Bratva Book 1

Lexi Asher

Copyright © 2023 Lexi Asher

All rights reserved. This copy is intended for the original purchaser of the book only. No part of this book may be reproduced, scanned, or distributed in any printed or electronic form, including recording, without prior written permission from the publisher, except for brief quotations in a book review.

This book is a work of fiction. Names, characters, places, and incidents either are products of the author's imagination or are used fictitiously. Any resemblance to actual persons, living or dead, events, or locales is entirely coincidental.

Contents

Chapter 1 - Reina

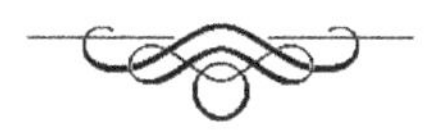

"Reina?" My assistant poked her head into my office. "Darla wants to see you as soon as you get a second."

I thanked her, and she slipped back to her desk. I told myself not to panic about Darla Talbot, owner of the Talbot Talent Agency, wanting to see me on a Friday afternoon. Should I jump up and run because she said as soon as I got a second? What if I had been really busy, wouldn't she want me to finish up my important work?

As it was, I didn't have anything for the rest of the day. My newest model and I had just returned from her first shoot, and she'd done such a good job I knew she wouldn't need babysitting from here on out. The photographer and I had a solid relationship, and he'd assured me he'd hire her again. The client, a vitamin brand, loved her as well. I didn't just sign people because they were beautiful, I made sure that they had solid work ethics as well. My commissions depended on my people showing up on time and getting rebooked.

Okay, so there was nothing wrong with any of my bookings, all my models were getting regular work, I'd been signing new talent. Why did Darla want to see me in her office? The owner of the agency wasn't the sort of boss that roamed the halls and mingled with us peons. She only showed up to schmooze with the biggest clients or the few really famous models we had. Or to chew someone out when they screwed up.

No, there was no reason I was in trouble. My reputation in this business was squeaky clean, and that was saying a lot considering the reputation of Talbot's wasn't exactly spotless. This was my first job straight out of college, and with no experience and even more importantly in this business, no connections, I'd felt grateful to be hired here at the time. Over the last year, I learned by the eye rolls and somewhat shady glances I got whenever I told someone else in the industry who I was with, Talbot's wasn't exactly the most revered talent agency in Miami. Still, it had been the only one offering me a job. It was such a competitive market down here in sunny Florida that we got more than our fair share of eager talent wanting to be signed and companies who would hire them for campaigns. I figured, in another couple of years, I could move on to a bigger agency.

There was absolutely no reason why I needed to be so anxious, as I made my way to Darla's giant corner office. I hyped myself up as I walked down the long halls that were lined with pictures of all our models and reminded myself of how many of them I had signed. Really, this was as good an opportunity as any to address some of the issues I'd been having, namely with my paychecks not reflecting the last few signing bonuses I should have received. And I needed to double check, but I was pretty sure my commissions were down when they should have been skyrocketing. My models were in high demand, and I hustled hard to keep them working.

Darla's assistant nodded for me to go in, but I tapped on the door anyway. Darla's voice came from the other side and I slipped in, a smile pasted on my face. Her laser eyes slowly swept from my shoes and worked their way up. I took in her sleek turquoise suit, a bright contrast to her dark red hair that was twisted up into a tight bun on the top of her head. Her bright red lips pursed as her gaze got to the top of my head. I kept my hands firmly at my sides to keep from checking my own dishwater blonde hair. It most certainly wasn't as perfectly arranged as hers, but it was fine. I hoped. As for my clothes, I wore my regular uniform of black jeans and a white silk blouse. Not flashy, but I wasn't in this business because of my looks. The only thing that could be considered really impressive were my sky high, embarrassingly expensive heels, my one and only weakness when it came to spending money. Darla didn't seem that impressed, though.

"Have a seat, Reina," she said.

I breathed a sigh of relief that she'd gotten my name right. Sadly, that wasn't always the case.

"How are you, Darla?" I asked.

She looked down at her tablet, but I could have sworn she rolled her eyes. "I don't have good news for you," she said, ignoring civilities and cutting to the chase. "I'm afraid we're letting you go."

"What?" I half stood in shock, especially after the major pep talk I'd given myself on the way here. "I don't understand. Why?"

Despite my shoe splurges now and then, I was a tightwad, pinching every penny. I made a good living at this job, but Miami Beach was expensive. My mind spun to my savings account, which wasn't very big, and my stomach turned over. I didn't love the Talbot Agency, but I loved my job and I couldn't afford to lose it.

She swiped a few times on her tablet, as if searching for the reason she was trying to ruin my life. "We expect a certain level of recruitment here. As you know, open call days rarely turn up any good faces, so we need our bookers and agents to bring people in."

I nodded vigorously. "Yes, and I do. I signed Melissa Angelo, who just did the Hartford Vitamins campaign this afternoon."

She frowned and swiped some more. "I'm showing Melissa was signed by Jimmy."

"No, that's wrong," I said so forcefully she looked up and raised an eyebrow.

I didn't care. Jimmy was a creep, always trying to get credit for others' work. A few of the other bookers had complained to me over drinks that they'd been swindled out of commissions because of him swooping in and claiming jobs, but since he was Darla's nephew, there was nothing they could do about it. I suddenly realized that he was probably the reason my pay had been so dismally bad the last few checks, when it should have been higher than ever due to all my hard work.

"Ask Melissa yourself," I said desperately, ignoring her increasing scowl.

She pushed her tablet over to me. "Here's her contract right here."

Well, this would solve it. I'd been there when she signed it. But it didn't solve anything because it was a completely new and different contract, with Jimmy listed as the signing agent.

"Then why was I the one going with her on her first job today?" I asked.

Darla shrugged. "I assumed Jimmy was delegating."

As if I were his subordinate, which I wasn't. I was fuming, and went numb as Darla listed off some of my other models who'd somehow been stolen by her nasty nephew. I knew how it had probably happened. He was a creep, but he was a handsome, rich creep, and he never let it be forgotten he was going to take over the agency one day. I could barely blame the young, hungry models for thinking they'd get a better deal if they sided with him over me, a nobody. Just someone who was willing to actually work for them, but still, a nobody. For all I knew, he was seducing them as well. I wouldn't put it past him, the creep.

But I couldn't defend myself or call her only, beloved nephew any names, so I accepted my dismissal as best I could. I certainly wasn't going to cry or beg, even if it would have made a difference, which it wouldn't. Darla was cold as ice and would never see the truth about Jimmy, even if it meant the ruination of her agency.

I kept it together. As soon as I was on my way home, I got on the phone to my oldest and best friend back in Kansas and let it rip.

"Oh my goodness," Lynn said through the speaker after my curse-filled tirade against the Talbot Agency. "That's awful."

"What's worse is it's going to be hell to find a new job. Nobody respects them so getting fired from there makes me seem like the ultimate loser."

"You're not any kind of loser, Reina. You'll get a new job."

"Ugh, I'm the worst," I said, sick of talking about my troubles. "How's Andrew? How's the peanut?"

Lynn married her high school sweetheart, our other best friend, Andrew, and now they were expecting their first child. I still couldn't wrap my head around the fact she was going to be a mom soon, at only twenty-three. I loved them both, they were the world's most perfect couple and would be great parents, but I couldn't imagine living their life at our age. As she rambled on about her doctor's appointments and cravings, and how sweet Andrew was being, I couldn't stop a microscopic kernel of envy. I quickly stomped it with a little internal laugh at myself. Of course I wanted a family one day. But far, far in the future. Without a job, that future was pushed even further down the line. I sighed deeply and Lynn stopped talking.

"You can always come back," she said, seeming to read my mind.

It would have been easier to go back to Kansas, definitely cheaper, but there was too much anguish there that I was free of here. A little more than a year ago, after my father's murder and the police bumbling that kept it unsolved, I couldn't take the memories, seeing him in all the places we used to go together and haunted by the fact he wasn't getting the justice he deserved. It was just us for the longest time since my mom died when I was only five. He was my rock and my hero, and being alone up there got to be too much for me. Miami held no such memories, so I was safe from ghosts here.

"You know I can't."

"Listen," she said, her take-charge tone in full effect. "We're not going to get maudlin or feel bad about ourselves. I suggest, no, I demand that you get yourself all fancied up and go out tonight. It's about time you take advantage of the famous Miami nightlife I always see on TV."

I snickered at her country bumpkin act. "I go out all the time."

"Pfft. To scout. I'm saying go out and drink and dance and find some guy to help you forget about Talbot's for a few hours. It's Friday, Reina. You can start fresh on Monday. Do it for me, so I can live vicariously."

I was shocked that Lynn, with her perfect life, might be a little envious of my mess, so I agreed I'd go out. We switched to video chat when I got back to my apartment and she helped me pick out an outfit, a slinky red dress I bought and never worked up the nerve to wear. It seemed like it was finally getting its tags removed and given a chance to make me shine. She wished me luck and I ended our three-hour-long call and headed out to get over a very bad day.

The club I chose was one I'd scouted at before. It was loud and packed and, thanks to my extremely revealing outfit, I had someone buy me a drink within minutes of hovering around the bar. I slammed back the first margarita and chatted with the out-of-state businessman for a few minutes while I sipped the second, but then as soon as he got distracted, I headed onto the dance floor. A few people I knew from the industry waved at me and I shouted greetings at them since it was obvious word hadn't gotten out that I wasn't at Talbot's anymore.

The alcohol started working its magic, and the heavy bass beat and the flashing lights took over. I forgot I wasn't tall and willowy like the models I was surrounded by all day and none of the men on the dance floor seemed to mind that I had ample curves, especially one man who sat in the VIP section just off the dance floor. Every time I turned in that direction our eyes seemed to lock. Was he going to be the guy to help me get over being fired today? A shot girl worked her way through the crowd, and I grabbed one, slamming it back before jumping back into the fray.

As I whirled and shimmied with the crowd, my attention kept getting drawn back to the man in the VIP section. How could it not, since he was basically a golden god, aloof on his velvet throne. Though he had a small crowd around him in the roped off area, he seemed set apart, like he really was a god. And I was really drunk, so I waved at him the next time we locked eyes.

A few minutes later, a big, muscly blond man took my arm. "Ivan would like your company," he yelled over the music.

I jerked my arm away. "Who?" I yelled back. He pointed and my golden god raised a hand. No smile, but he lifted an eyebrow. Was he actually summoning me? The intense stare he was casting my way oozed confidence and control. My insides wobbled, thrown off kilter by the way he seemed to devour me with his eyes. I turned back to his drone and laughed. "Well, tell him, if he wants my company, he can come out here and get it himself."

The man looked stunned, but I danced away from him, not a care in the world. Music and margaritas were my new best friends so who needed a man? The next time I turned around, my golden god was right there in front of me, looming over me, in fact. Holy crap, he was handsome up close. Like he was carved from ice, chiseled jaw and cheekbones, stormy, sea-blue eyes that went straight through me. His golden blond hair that made me give him his nickname fell in soft waves over his forehead and curled around his ears. Who needed a man? Me. This man.

I wanted to take some time to really check out the rest of him, but before I knew it, he had his arm wrapped around my waist, and I was pinned against his big, hard body. Yep, as muscular as he looked from his throne.

He kept me held tight to him despite it being a fast song, and I stared up at him, intoxicated by his beauty and hard body, and just plain intoxicated to boot. He licked his lower lip, as he leaned closer to me and

I melted. My legs actually went weak. I grabbed his shoulders to keep from swaying and eagerly accepted his rough kiss. Oh, yes, this was going to be the man who made me forget I got fired.

Chapter 2 - Ivan

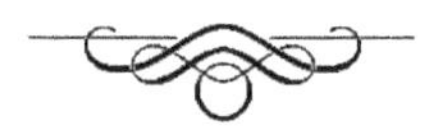

I got to my club, one of my legit businesses, and saw something that darkened my mood, and my mood wasn't great, to begin with. I went there to check on things, but also to unwind, have a few drinks, and oversee one of the lighter sides of my empire. One of the legal sides.

Which was why I nearly lost it when I saw one of my bartenders selling something other than alcohol from behind the bar. I thought I could trust this young man, had given him extra jobs to do that were very lucrative for him, and this was how he repaid me?

With a snap, I sent my cousin Dmitri to retrieve the illicit substance from the girl he'd sold it to, then had my other cousin, Maksim go search his locker.

"Bring him to me," I told my younger brother and second in command, Aleksei, then headed to the back to see if anything turned up in the employee lounge.

Maksim had cut the padlock off the locker and pulled out a treasure trove of things I didn't want in my club. I slammed my hand into the locker, denting the metal. I don't like being taken for a fool, or betrayed. This seemed like both of those things. Maksim looked pityingly over my shoulder, and I turned to see Aleksei hauling in the bartender.

"I don't get what's—" His glib voice cut off as he saw his stash revealed, and the smile fell off his face.

"I don't expect that you can explain this," I said. If he didn't lie to me, he'd live. The thing I hate more than being taken for a fool and betrayed, is a liar. "But why don't you try."

"I have no idea what that is," he said, sweat dotting his forehead. "I'm not the only one who uses that locker."

"You weren't selling these pills to a young lady a few minutes ago?" I asked, keeping my hands loose, my voice calm. When he caught my eyes, he withered, seeming to shrink a few inches. I've been told I can act as calm as I want, but my eyes always gave me away.

"What? No, of course not," he said, inadvertently taking a step back. Aleksei and Maksim took a step forward. "Ivan, you know me—"

I raised a brow. "Mr. Morozov," I said coldly. After all, our family name meant frost. "You're honestly telling me you were not selling drugs in my establishment?"

He looked hopeful, the poor soul. "Absolutely not. Believe me, I'm aware of your rules about this."

"So you think I'm either stupid or blind?"

"Of course not, Mr. Morozov."

Behind him, my brother rolled his eyes. He was clearly telling me I'd given the bartender enough chances, and he wasn't going to confess. A confession wouldn't have saved him from punishment. But it might have saved his life.

"Take him away and deal with him," I said.

I turned away as Aleksei and Maksim dragged him out, blocking out the sound of his pathetic pleading. Now I was down a bartender, but he'd be quickly replaced. My club was one of the most popular in South Beach, and it was jam-packed every night, but especially on the weekends. Now that the unpleasant business was taken care of, I could enjoy it.

I decided to sit close to the dance floor in hopes the throbbing beats would shake my foul mood, and my employees quickly set up a VIP section for me. My brother returned with a few of our other associates, and the women they chose to entertain, and they crowded behind the ropes to find seats on the velvet sofas. I chose to sit apart from them, not in any mood for idle chat yet. Aleksei leaned close to tell me that Maksim and Dmitri were taking care of the bartender situation.

"We'll keep it under wraps," he said, getting settled on one of the couches and accepting a drink from the server assigned to us.

I leaned back in my big chair facing the dance floor, ready to survey this small part of my kingdom.

"No," I said. "It's better that the others find out what he did and the consequences for it. I can't keep out all the riff-raff, but I can keep my employees under control at least."

He nodded, even though I could see he didn't completely agree with me. My brother was my staunchest supporter, and the one I most often butted heads with. It was a tenuous power dance, but I was the oldest, the heir. I was born to lead and in the end, he always remembered his place. Our two other brothers were currently out of town on business, and they were much easier to keep in line. Once word got out about why this bartender had "quit" suddenly, people would remember things. Put two and two together about past disappearances and recall that the Morozov family is not to be trifled with.

My decision to sit by the dance floor paid off, and my mood improved when I saw a stunning young woman dancing with abandon in the middle of the crowded space. Her dark blonde hair swung around her shoulders, and her red dress seemed painted to her lush curves. Every time someone blocked my view of her I had to resist getting up and shoving them out of the way. When she kept looking over at me, her cheeks rosy from exertion and her eyes bright in the flashing lights, my cock twitched to life. I wasn't planning on a rendezvous since it had been a grueling week, but that was before that curvy princess danced into my life. And I'd have her in my life, at least for tonight.

I turned and snapped for Maksim's attention. "Bring that luscious blonde to me," I ordered, watching as he dutifully made his way through the crush to my princess. My mood was getting better and better.

Until he returned alone, a stony look on his face. "She said to go out there yourself." He tried to hide his smirk, but failed.

With a snarl, I kept watching her. How dare she? She must not be a regular, so therefore she didn't know I owned the place. Most women jumped at the chance behind the VIP ropes, a chance at gaining some little part of my empire. There was never a challenge to getting a woman's company for a night, and I normally liked it that way.

The more I watched her shake her sexy ass, the more I liked the fact she wasn't impressed with me, yet. Maybe I was up for a challenge, after all. My cock was certainly urging me to get out there. When she threw her head back and sinuously ran her hands down the sides of her curvy waist, I stood without thinking and stomped toward the dance floor.

When her body was flush with mine, I wasn't disappointed with the close up view. She was beautiful, almost angelic, with cherry lips and big brown eyes, like an innocent doe. But the way she ground against me wasn't innocent at all, and my body reacted like a match to kerosene. I buried my fingers in her hair and tilted her head back. Our eyes met and she grabbed for me as I crashed my mouth to hers. Her tongue tasted of strawberries and tequila. I'd order her more margaritas when I got her back to my table, after I threw everyone else out so I could have her to myself.

She writhed against me, her grip tight on my shoulders as my hands roamed her body. "Come back to my table," I commanded.

She laughed, sliding her hands down my chest. I grabbed them and held them tight, guiding her off the dance floor. With a snap, my guests cleared out and I pulled my pretty princess down onto the velvet couch with me.

"Tell me your name, Princess," I said, tucking some of her blonde curls behind her ear and trailing my finger down the side of her throat to the thin shoulder strap of her dress.

She shivered at my touch and blinked up at me. "Reina," she answered.

My hand trailed lower, down her arm, my thumb grazing her full breast. Her skin was softer than the finest silk. "Ah, not a princess, then, but a queen."

She leaned close, putting her hand on my thigh. "And what's your name, Golden God?"

I burst out laughing at her nickname and her cheeks flamed to match her dress.

"Oh no, did I say that out loud?"

"You did, my queen," I told her. "But I don't mind it. A queen and a god are a perfect match. My name is Ivan, though, if you prefer to call me that."

"Okay, Ivan." Her smile was irresistible and I wanted to give her anything she desired.

"Tell me your greatest wish and I'll make it happen," I said rashly.

Still, I knew I'd give her whatever she asked for. She furrowed her brow and seemed to give it some serious thought. I realized I wanted her so badly I'd wake up the nearest jeweler and shower her in diamonds if that was what she requested. It was unprecedented, the way she made me feel.

"You know what I really want?" She leaned back and sighed, locking those doe eyes with mine. I was hooked, and breathlessly waited to hear what she asked for.

Chapter 3 - Reina

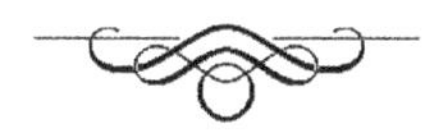

This guy really had me hot and bothered, with his searing looks and roaming hands. He literally swept me off my feet for a moment out on the dance floor and now he was acting like he owned the place, making everyone leave the VIP area with a snap of his fingers so we could be alone. I had to admit it was impressive.

The way he was looking at me, like I was the most delicious meal he'd been waiting all day for, didn't hurt either. I leaned away from his kisses, far stronger than the potent shots I was taking, and planted my hands on his rock-hard chest. He was huge, an absolute mountain of muscle, and his icy blue gaze should have given me chills, not tremors of desire. He wanted to know my greatest wish? Hmm, that could get interesting.

But, actually, I realized I was starving, having skipped dinner due to my mood from getting fired. I didn't let reality sneak back in. I slid my hand up through his hair.

"I'd kill for a Reynaldo's Cuban sandwich."

He stared at me for a second before bursting out laughing. "A Cuban sandwich?"

I nodded and he snapped for someone hovering outside the roped off area, told him something, then turned his attention back to me. I couldn't hear what he was saying in the man's ear, but Ivan's hand moved slowly from my knee up my thigh, not stopping when it hit the edge of my short dress. With a sigh, the source of my hunger changed, and I shifted closer so he could kiss me again.

"Yes, this is what I'm really hungry for," I murmured as his mouth crashed against mine.

He pulled away long enough to chuckle, a low rumble that shot straight through me. "Then you'll have it and more."

That 'and more' was very interesting. I wrapped my arms around his neck and let him tug me half onto his lap. Forgetting about the crowd all around us, the only thing that mattered at that moment was Ivan's fiery touch and the feel of his tongue invading my mouth. His hands slid up my back to tangle in my hair, pulling my head back to nibble his way down my neck. If anyone was gaping at us, I didn't care one bit. He didn't seem to either, because he wasn't stingy at all in giving me what I craved.

I was dizzy and writhing against him when someone tapped his shoulder. I blinked to see his fierce glare at the man standing behind him with a greasy paper bag in his hand. He relaxed and took the bag, turning to me. Why were we stopping?

"Your feast has arrived, my queen."

The nickname should have sounded like a joke to me, along with the ravenous way his eyes couldn't seem to stop moving up and down my body. I wasn't used to this kind of attention from any man, least of all someone with Ivan's amazing looks and obvious power. He acted like he owned this place and yet, he chose me. And for whatever reason, I could tell he was being sincere. There was just something about him I could feel in my gut. Or maybe I was feeling it in other, less trustworthy places of my anatomy, especially after the way he'd been stroking me. When he ripped open the bag and began unwrapping a Cuban sandwich, my jaw dropped.

"You really meant it when you said you'd get me whatever I wanted," I said, stunned.

His hands stilled, and he looked at me deliberately. "I mean everything I say."

His stone cold voice sent a frisson of nerves down my spine. Was I letting my body, which was way too full of alcohol, get me in trouble? Then he broke off a piece of the sandwich and very adorably held it out to me. This was what I needed after being trampled down by Darla and Jimmy. I needed to be treated like a queen by a gorgeous, golden god. I parted my lips for the bite. His eyes wouldn't let me look anywhere but at him.

I finally broke the spell and laughed nervously. "I should have aimed higher than a sandwich," I joked.

"You can keep asking me for anything," he said.

Unnerved, I reached the little table in front of us and split the meal in half. "I'd like it if you shared this with me. You can't keep feeding me like that."

He raised a brow that told me he could do whatever he wanted, and I squeezed my thighs together at the heat his intense gaze had shooting through me. I tore off a piece and held it to his lips with my own impatient look. With a laugh, he gobbled up the bite, grabbing my hand to kiss my fingers before letting me go.

I asked him where he was from. "I can't place your accent," I explained. "It's very faint, but it's there."

"I was born in Russia, came here when I was ten years old. Took over my father's business."

I briefly thought about asking him where he worked and if he was hiring but shoved my situation to the backburner again. I wasn't going to let anything ruin this fairy tale I was currently in. Exactly never in my life had such a man treated me like this, and I meant to enjoy every second. I told him I was also a transplant to Miami, and how I came here for my first job out of college. I expected him to politely ask where I went to school, but he took my chin and locked eyes with me again.

"There's something bothering you, Reina," he said.

I got another shiver. How did he know? It was like he could see inside me, his lake blue eyes diving into my thoughts, my soul, even. It was scarily intense, but I kind of liked it. I started to shrug him off and assure him everything was fine, but those eyes were commanding me to tell him the truth.

For whatever reason, I blurted out everything about the mess at the modeling agency, the humiliation of being fired unfairly. "Since I'm not related to the owner, there was nothing I could do. I packed up my things and made the walk of shame out of there, flanked by a security guard," I finished, fighting back the tears I barely kept back that afternoon.

"Ah, yes, I know all too well about nepotism," he said, after I spilled my guts.

"Then you know there was nothing I could do, since that asshat Jimmy Talbot is going to take over the place when Darla retires in a few years."

"I've had dealings with Talbot Talent Agency," he said, shaking his head. "You should count yourself lucky not to be involved with them anymore."

"I guess," I sighed. "But I'm still out of a job, and I did love it, except for…"

"That asshat Jimmy Talbot," he said darkly.

I laughed at his murderous look on my behalf. It was nice to be able to commiserate with someone who was so clearly on my side. He didn't join in my laughter, he was too busy dropping his gaze to my chest. The food was done, and I wanted dessert.

"Thanks for listening to me complain," I said, pulling myself back onto his lap.

Who was I tonight? Brazenly straddling the hottest man at the club as if I didn't have a care in the world. When his hands circled my waist and I felt his stiff bulge beneath me, I leaned over him and nipped his full lower lip. He gripped me tighter, and I ground against him.

"I want something else now," I said.

"Tell me," he growled. "I'll give you anything you want."

I pushed my fingers into his hair and lowered my lips to his. "You know," I told him, feeling his hot breath mingle with mine.

His answer was silent, his lips claiming mine.

Chapter 4 - Ivan

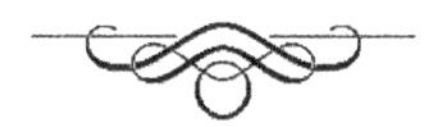

I had to have her. This curvy beauty with sadness in her eyes. I knew there was more to it than just losing her job and my need to make everything right in her world was only overshadowed when she pulled her lush body onto my lap and wriggled her hot pussy all over my hard cock.

She was like fire, melting me to my very soul. There was no way she wasn't coming home with me tonight. It was unironically a matter of life or death at that point. At the sound of her moan, I broke our feverish kiss and picked her up, carrying her through the club.

"Where are we going?" she asked, her breath against my neck making me harder.

"Somewhere more private," I told her. As much as I wanted to take her then and there, up against the nearest wall, I knew I needed to take my time with my queen.

"That's a good idea." She wrapped her arms around me trustingly and tipped her head back to smile at me.

Despite the crazed lust she ignited in me, I took note of where my men were. My brother Aleksei was chatting with someone at the bar, and he nodded briefly when I caught his eye. He'd stay until closing to make sure there was no backlash over the bartender. I'd send someone out to investigate higher up that food chain tomorrow, to make sure whoever was supplying him knew to knock it off in my establishments. Maksim was standing sentinel at the backdoor and I paused to hear what he had to say.

"Taken care of," he grunted, careful to keep his eyes on me and not the woman in my arms.

"Good. Don't bother me anymore tonight," I answered, holding Reina closer as I pushed out the back door to where my driver was waiting.

"Do you run this place?" she asked.

"I own it," I told her, cutting off any more questions with a kiss.

She sighed against my mouth and straddled me again as soon as we were in the car. I tapped on the glass and we headed toward my apartment here on South Beach, since it was the closest. The way she was grinding on me, I might have had to take her there in the car.

"I should have my seatbelt on." She slid away and I grabbed her back, planting my hands firmly on each side of her ripe ass.

"You should stay right here," I told her, leaning to lick down the side of her neck to the swell of her tits heaving over the top of her tight dress. "God, you're gorgeous." My cock responded when she gave me a dazzling smile.

"I can tell you mean that," she said, running her fingers through my hair.

I frowned. "Of course I do. I don't lie, Reina. Everything I tell you will always be the truth."

She shivered and I rubbed the goosebumps from her arms, then leaned over to adjust the air conditioning. She stopped me, her eyes wide.

"I'm not cold. You make me a little nervous."

I should have made her nervous, but that wasn't what I wanted. I stopped rubbing her arms and lightly trailed my fingers up and down them instead, leaning close to taste her cherry lips. No, strawberry, but sweeter and juicier. "I don't want to make you nervous, my queen. I want to make you feel good."

She wriggled on my lap, her eyes closed and lips parted for my tongue to delve between. "It's working," she sighed.

The moment it pulled to a stop in the parking garage, I carried her out of the car. With a laugh, she held on tight as the elevator took us to my penthouse suite. Once inside, I settled her feet back down on the floor, her body gliding against mine. She seemed to fit me perfectly as she melted into my arms. I guided her to the wall of windows overlooking the darkened water.

"I love the ocean," she said, her eyes intent on the lights of a cruise ship off in the distance. "It's so beautiful."

The way she was looking at the view was the way I felt looking at her. Wistful, and almost reverent. I swept her from her tousled blonde hair down her curvy body, her smooth, tanned legs, all the way to her sky high, fuck-me heels, and slowly made the journey up again, settling on her profile as she continued to watch the ship make its way out to sea.

"Just like you," I said.

Her lips curled into a smile and she turned. "I could get used to the way you talk," she said. "Your words, your accent." She made her own visual trip up and down my body, reaching out to take my shoulders.

I knew I could get used to the way she was looking at me, and pulled her close. She gasped when her body collided with my stiff cock, and I tugged her hair back to claim her mouth.

"My little queen, you taste like strawberries," I said. "Like the summer itself."

Something I've always loved despite so many complaints about it, was the heat of Florida's long summers. I remembered the harsh winters of my childhood—that cold was stuck in my bones' memory. Reina was hot and sweet like my favorite season. She moaned in answer, her tongue dancing with mine in perfect rhythm, just as we'd danced at the club. I pulled away and picked her up again, this time settling her on the nearby granite countertop. I needed more. "I want to taste you everywhere."

Her eyes dilated, and her legs spread, as I pulled her to the edge and dipped between her silky thighs. My stubble rasped against her leg, as I dragged my lips to the edge of her panties, already damp from her desire. I uttered a curse in my native tongue, as I yanked them aside and plunged my face into her juicy pussy.

Her fingers ripped through my hair, pushing my head further, then gasping as she tried to drag it away. I slowed my fevered licking to gently circle her swollen clit, gripping her hips to tame her wild bucking. God, she was responsive to my slightest touch. It was a miracle I was hanging on. She was so open and ready for me; my cock screamed to have her right there and then. But the look on her face when I glanced up at her, mouth open, full of rapture, made me want to hear her scream first. I plunged my tongue deep inside her wet folds, in and out the way my cock longed to, stroking her slit and nibbling at her tender nub until her legs went tight around my shoulders and her breath expelled in a high-pitched wheeze.

"Oh my God, Ivan," she cried, grasping at my hair. "Oh. My. God."

I snickered, thinking of her little nickname for me, even though it seemed like I was the one doing the worshiping at the moment. And still I kept lavishing her delectable pussy.

When she collapsed backwards on the counter, her hands going limp to lie at her sides, I relented, nipping at her as I worked my way up her belly to her mouth. I wanted to kiss her with her juices on my lips.

"Tell me you want more, Reina," I said. A command, or a plea? My hand slid between her thighs and cupped her still pulsing sex.

She kissed me hard, panting from the orgasm I gave her. "I want more. Please. So much more."

I grabbed her up and backed us toward my bedroom, my fingers tight in her soft flesh, bursting to feel her skin against my palms.

By the time the backs of my legs hit the side of my bed, her dress was up around her waist, her panties lost somewhere along the way and good riddance to them. I couldn't contain a groan of pleasure as I cupped her sweet ass. Her arms tightened around my neck, her breath hitching as she frantically kissed my neck. She wrapped her legs around my waist and squeezed as if I'd ever let her go.

"Ivan," she whispered, the heat of her breath making me hold her tighter.

"I won't let go," I promised, falling backwards.

She tumbled with me to land on my chest, and I rolled us to the side. "You're redeeming what was a really bad day," she said as her innocent eyes searched mine and a smile wreathed her pretty face.

I found I was looking forward to each upward tilt of her full lips, craving those smiles. Recalling how badly she'd been treated at her former job hit me with a blast of fury as I ran my fingers through her hair. I'd make things right for her, I had that power.

But right now, my hand settled in between her thighs again, her soft moan making me forget my anger.

"Let's finish it off with a bang, shall we?" I suggested.

She gasped when I slipped my fingers into her wet heat, then smiled down at me. "That's why you're the boss," she said with a wicked smile that had my cock pulsing.

I dragged my fingers out of her wet heat and grabbed her hips, sinking my fingers into the ample flesh as she sunk her body onto me. My blissful groan had her looking smugly down at me, but I didn't mind her little bit of arrogance. It was well deserved, and I'd be making her scream again soon enough.

She rode me hard, and I enjoyed the view as her heavy tits bounced and she threw her head back so that her hair fell against the arching curve of her spine. My hands roamed with a mind of their own as my cock greedily took everything she gave.

I reached to tweak her taut nipples, running my hands down her sides to grip her waist. "You deserve your title, my queen."

Leaning down, her nipples brushed my chest and her lips dragged from my jaw to my earlobe. "I'll reign over your big cock any day," she breathed huskily.

Pulling back, her cheeks were pink and her eyes wide, as if she couldn't believe she'd said it. I laughed even as my balls contracted tight against her.

"Ah, we'll see about that," I said, flipping her easily onto her back. "It's my turn, now."

I came down smoothly between her lush thighs, my cock ramming deep into her. Both our moans mingled as our mouths collided. Her tight channel locked around my shaft was the most delicious pain, transporting me in a way I didn't recognize. Who was this woman to make me feel this rapturous? As much as I wanted to take my own pleasure from her perfect body, I had to see her come, watch those doe eyes roll back and those plump lips fall open as I made her lose control.

Her gasps punctuated my hard thrusts, and I eased back, sliding my fingers between us, never taking my eyes off her gorgeous face. She blinked, focusing on me as I found her clit, and her legs tightened around my hips.

"Oh yes, Ivan," she sighed. I'd known her for a few hours and I already lived for those soft breaths. "Right there…"

I watched her forget where she was, forget everything but the pure pleasure I coaxed with my fingertips. Then I forgot everything as her tight pussy clenched around my shaft, and her scream filled my ears. With another thrust I was spent, filling her with my seed. I collapsed against her, our sweat mingling. She said something unintelligible, and I answered something just as inane. We both laughed, and she buried her face in my neck.

"Best day ever."

I was in complete agreement, surprised she transported me so easily from my own problems and glad I'd made her forget hers. "My little queen, it's only just begun," I promised.

I woke up to the sun shining brightly through the blinds. I was too busy to close them the night before, with all my attention on Reina. Pesky reality threatened to take over my thoughts with this new day, urging me to get up and face it. Not yet. I didn't bother reaching for the remote to close them, reaching for my queen instead. I should have been sated from our passionate night, and should have been drained dry. But I couldn't seem to get enough of her, and my cock was ready for round… I'd lost count. This was a new day. We could start a fresh count.

My hand slid across cool, empty sheets. Only her scent lingered on the pillows. The bathroom door was wide open and my apartment was as quiet as a tomb. She was gone, sneaking away while I slept. Disappointment washed over me, stronger than the fierce morning sun. I told myself it was only because I wanted to fuck her again, but there was something else there, something I didn't much care for.

My phone buzzed from across the room, and I got up to see who was bothering me at this ungodly hour. It had to be one of my brothers. No one else would dare. Sure enough, it was Aleksei.

"What?" I answered harshly.

"I'm sorry if you're not alone," he said, grinding my disappointment in further. "But we've got problems."

"I am alone, and we've always got problems." Despite my flippant tone, I sat down for whatever he had to tell me.

Being the most powerful crime family in Miami came with its share of annoyances as well as all the perks. Someone always wanted one of us dead, with me being the main target. I'd been dodging threats since I was sixteen, after our father died and left me in charge. He himself had been fearless in the face of any foe, and he'd left me well-trained. I finished bringing up my younger brothers to be just as tough, so when one of them told me there was a problem, I took them seriously.

"It's the bartender."

"I thought he was taken care of," I said. "Maksim told me himself that it was handled." I trusted no one completely, but our cousins, Maksim and Dmitri, got as close to my total confidence as anyone in our organization.

"The bartender was taken care of, but it's deeper than that, Ivan." He let out a long breath, as if dreading what he had to say next.

"Spit it out," I ordered.

"He wasn't acting on his own."

Damn it. I hadn't thought so, especially after I saw the size of the stash in his locker. "Tell me it was some low-level nobody." I already knew the answer. Aleksei wouldn't be calling me, his voice full of worry, if that was the case. His silence spoke volumes. "Tell me it isn't the Balakins."

"We believe it's the Balakins," he finally said.

I held away the phone and swore viciously. "Will they never learn?"

"Apparently not."

I ordered him to round up our brothers and meet me as soon as they returned. It was time to put a stop to these upstarts, trying to take what was mine. What I'd earned, and I meant to keep. Even if it meant war.

Chapter 5 - Reina

When insatiable Ivan finally fell asleep, I was tempted to stay tucked against his chest and join him in dreamland. Still tingling and giddy from the hours of ecstasy he treated me to, it took all my willpower to get out of his bed. As I tiptoed through his lux penthouse apartment and took in one last look at the stunning ocean view with the sun just peeking over the horizon, I knew his life and mine were utterly incompatible. He was a rich club owner who probably had a different woman over every night. I was an out-of-work, small-town girl who didn't have time to get her heart broken by a sexy Russian player. It was for the best to keep this a perfect one-night stand.

I gave up trying to find my panties and with a final look at the sleeping golden god, I crept out the door and down the elevator. The minute I was back in my own modest apartment, I chugged a huge glass of water and fell into bed, drifting off to sleep with Ivan's spicy scent still on my skin along with the lingering feel of his hands.

When I woke up, I called Lynn to tell her everything. It showed how out of character my little tryst was when she hollered for Andrew to come hear the details with her.

"So Reina finally got laid in Miami," he said while she laughed.

"Are we still in high school?" I asked, thinking back to when the three of us were in a race to lose our virginity. Lynn and Andrew won it in a tie during senior year when they realized they were madly in love with one another. At the time I'd been terrified they'd have a nasty breakup, and I'd have to choose sides, but they were every bit as crazy about each other now as they were then.

I stuffed down my embarrassment and spilled almost all of the details, not having to exaggerate Ivan's good looks or impressive wealth one bit.

"Our girl's all grown up," Andrew said with a mock sniffle.

"Reina, he sounds amazing," Lynn said. I heard her shooing Andrew away so we could speak more seriously, and she asked when I was going to see him again.

"Never," I assured her.

"What?" she shrieked. "You need to get your butt back to his club again tonight and bag that trophy."

I wished we were on video chat so she could see my look of horror. "Since when did you get so mercenary?" I asked.

"Since realizing how expensive doctor visits and baby stuff is."

Lynn worked as an elementary school teacher and Andrew worked for his father's solar panel company so I knew they made a pretty good living, but I understood her stress with all the changes coming up in her life.

"Still, I'm not bagging anyone," I said.

"But you just gave me a bunch of delicious details about how perfect he was."

I closed my eyes and let myself relive some of those memories again, then shook my head. "It's better to let it stay perfect. Trying to recreate it would be folly."

"You're an idiot," she said.

"Yes, but you love me. Goodbye."

I ended the call to her laughter, but I didn't want to hear her cajoling me into seeking out Ivan again. I needed to get my life back on track before it was too far off the rails and haunting his club in hopes he'd take notice of me again wasn't part of the plan. In truth, I didn't think my ego could take it if he'd gotten his fill of me. It was better to keep it perfect like I told Lynn.

I fired up my computer to start updating my resumé and scrolled the local news for a few minutes to try to get past my dread over looking for a new job. The mild anxious feeling was replaced with shock when I saw one of the headlines was about Jimmy, of all people.

Prominent Modeling Agent Victim of Violent Attack.

I was too shocked to roll my eyes at the news outlet calling him prominent, and clicked on the article. There wasn't much, just that he'd been out with one of Talbot's models and had been viciously beaten. He had numerous broken bones and was currently hospitalized in serious condition. I recognized the model's name, since she was one I'd signed even though, if I were able to comb through Talbot's records, I would have bet money that Jimmy was credited for it. I scrolled through my phone and found her number.

"It's Reina Hall," I said when she answered. "Are you all right? I saw the news just now."

"Oh my God, Reina," she said. "It was awful, but I'm fine. We were coming out of a restaurant last night down on South Beach and these two men cornered us on a little side street. They told me to turn and face the wall and I swear I thought I was about to be shot, but they never laid a finger on me." Her voice broke. "But they really laid into Jimmy."

"You couldn't identify them at all to the police?"

"No, they had on masks and kept their heads down before they made me turn around. They had strange accents, but I couldn't place them. Maybe some kind of European."

I made a disgusted noise. "The things people do for a little bit of money."

"That's the strange thing," she said. "They didn't take anything from either of us, and you've probably seen Jimmy wears a Rolex."

I suppressed a grumble. Yes, I'd seen it. He couldn't do anything without ostentatiously waving it around. Well, having a cast on his arm might keep him from doing that for a while. Was that too unkind? Not that he'd ever shown me any kindness, or even basic decency. I wished her well and told her I was glad she was okay.

"Sorry you won't be working at Talbot's anymore," she said.

I ended the call. Maybe if she and some of the other models hadn't given in to Jimmy's dubious charms and switched loyalties, she wouldn't have to be sorry. Ivan was right; I was better off without that lousy agency and their unethical practices. I wondered what he'd have to say if he knew about this, after I'd talked his ear off at the club last night about how awful Jimmy was. It was a funny coincidence. Funny if Jimmy hadn't been hurt so badly, that was.

I shrugged as I found my resumé, ready to start the slog of looking for a new job. I didn't need to feel bad about what happened to that rat. As far as I was concerned, he got what he deserved. I chalked up my stunning lack of sympathy to the fact it was his fault I needed to find a new job in the first place.

Six Weeks Later

I found a new job—as a barista. I knew I should be grateful to have work at all, and I was happy to still be in Miami. I loved it here. But I came here to rise up in the ranks of the modeling business, with the endgame of running my own agency one day in the far off, hazy future. I didn't want to be here if I was just scraping by.

I had resumés out at every agency in town, and even put a few calls into people at smaller markets up north in Tampa and Orlando. I considered those places less than ideal since there just wasn't as much work as here in Miami, so it was a real blow when no one wanted me there, either. I suspected my reputation had been poisoned either by Darla or Jimmy himself, but I struggled not to be bitter about it. I was good at my job. Well, not the barista one. I downright sucked at that and hated it, but I was a good talent booker. I was going to give it a few more months of calls and meetings before I packed it in and went home to Kansas.

I really didn't want to pack it in. I still couldn't bear all the memories there, good and bad alike. And the bitterness with the incompetent police who didn't seem to try at all to find Dad's killer had been eating me alive. I could barely function and had a bad feeling that the whole cycle would start again if I was back in that environment.

Steam billowed over the top of the cup of cappuccino I was preparing and scalded my hand. I barely kept from spilling the whole thing and blinked back tears as I handed it over to the customer. My replacement was late and I'd been on my aching feet for over eight hours. On top of that, I'd been feeling sick for the last several days. It had been getting progressively worse, sneaking up on me at all hours of the day and making me run for the bathroom to spew whatever I'd managed to eat. Right now I was alternating between starving and barely keeping my roiling stomach under control.

When my replacement came running in, full of apologies, I barely acknowledged her before getting the heck out of there. At home, I lay listlessly on the couch trying to keep the canned chicken soup down. I finally called Lynn to complain. I'd been putting on a brave face and pretending everything was fine, but I was never great at being sick so needed to whine.

"I've been barfing almost nonstop," I told her. "I thought it was a twenty-four-hour bug, then a forty-eight-hour bug, but now it's been almost a week. And I'm tired and irritable and—"

"Do your boobs hurt?" she interrupted.

I snorted. "What?" But I squeezed my arms across my chest, realizing I was a bit tender. "Oh shit, no."

"Take a pregnancy test, pronto. Right now."

"I don't keep those lying around the house, Lynn," I snapped, taking my horror out on her.

"Go get one and call me back the second you know."

I sat there staring blankly at my phone for the longest time after she hung up on me. She was crazy, she had to be. Then I thought back to that wild night with Ivan. Even through my anxiety I couldn't help but smile at the memory. It had been hard not going back for more, but then I got so busy with my crappy new job and trying to get a better one that I mostly forgot about him.

Talk about an amazing night of pure, unadulterated passion. A whole lot of passion. And I'd been pretty drunk, so I really had no recollection of whether or not he used a condom. Certainly not every time, if at all. My cheeks burned with shame at the stupidity. Ignoring the newest bout of nausea, I raced to the corner store and bought up a variety of different pregnancy tests, not sure which were the best brands.

They were all either great or awful, because they all turned up the same result. I called Lynn back.

"Positive," I croaked.

"This is fine," she said.

"Not really." I slumped against the edge of the tub in my tiny bathroom. I lived in a one room apartment. My bed was also my couch.

There was no room for a baby here, and I couldn't afford a bigger place with my current wages. "I guess I'm coming home," I said dully. "I certainly can't raise a kid on my own here."

"What about Ivan?" she asked.

"What about him?"

She sucked in a breath. "You have to tell him. Even if you're going to be stubborn and not accept help and even if he's an asshole who doesn't want any part of it, he has a right to know."

I groaned, knowing she was right. "Fine. I'll try to find him at his club tonight and tell him."

I just prayed he'd remember me.

Chapter 6 - Ivan

It was still early, right before we opened the doors of the club, and I sat at one of the empty tables with Aleksei, who had his head in his hands. The servers bustled around, getting things ready for that night's crowd but they were lost in their own worlds or were smart enough not to try too hard to listen in on our conversation. I liked coming here for meetings if they weren't of the utmost confidentiality. The way the strobe lights circled despite the house lights still being on, casting red and blue lights across Aleksei's harried face, kept things from seeming out of control. And things weren't out of control, no matter how worried my brother was.

I didn't worry, I took care of things. I took care of it when the Balakins were encroaching on this place, my second home, my legitimate business, with their dirty drug dealing, and I would take care of whatever Aleksei was having so much trouble telling me.

"Just spit it out," I told him. "What's got you looking like someone kicked your puppy?"

He scowled at me, because that was a real thing that happened to him. When he was only eight and we'd just arrived here in America, our father had given him a slobbering yellow lab pup to keep him from being too sad about leaving our home. Dmitri had kicked the annoying thing, and Aleksei had been in a spitting rage. My father told him to stop flailing and shouting and get the justice he needed for his dog. That was the first time my brother ever beat the hell out of someone. Our ten-year-old cousin had to have a nose job after that, which we still teased him about.

It took a lot to make my slow-to-anger brother mad enough to get violent, and he was still that way today, but he loved that dog. The only times I saw him cry were when our father died and when the dog died his junior year of high school.

He drew in a breath. "It's the Balakins again. They've been collecting protection money."

"Then we'll need to recoup those funds and teach them the error behind thinking they could do that." I cracked my knuckles and shook my head, not finding the flashing strobe lights so comforting and whimsical anymore. This was a flagrant act of disrespect, especially after we'd gone so easy on them after the drug incident. Probably *because* we'd gone so easy on them. "We need to come down hard this time, Aleksei. No more of your diplomacy."

"I still feel we can find a way to join forces with them," he said. "We're all Russians. We're all Bratva."

I slammed my hand down on the table, making it shake. "We may all be Russians, but we are not all Bratva, Aleksei. You must remember that."

He put his head in his hands again with a groan, working up to arguing with me, but knowing me well enough to know he'd lose. I knew him well enough to know he'd still try and waited to hear him out. There was a commotion by the bar, and I heard a raised, feminine voice that made me stand up to see what it was all about. I'd spent the last several weeks dealing with the fallout from the Balakin problem, but that voice still snuck into my memory from time to time. Now it wasn't soft and breathy in my ear, but agitated. I must have been mistaken, just hopeful to see her again. I called for the bouncers to stand aside, and there she stood, small but fiery, her fists clenched at her sides.

Reina, my little runaway queen.

She wore jeans that hugged her rounded hips and the sense memory of them curled my fingers as if I was still holding her tight. Her chest heaved beneath her frilly white tank top and her eyes were filled with tears.

That hit me like a brick to the side of the head, and yes, I'd actually had the misfortune to experience that.

"Let her in," I barked, then turned to Aleksei. "We'll finish discussing this later. Maybe much later."

He looked at Reina, then back at me with an eye roll, but left, probably glad not to have to get in a fight with me for now. I waved Reina over, unable to take my eyes off her as she came toward me. For whatever reason, she'd stuck with me, unlike any other woman before or since as I'd tried to erase the taste and smell of her, and I was happy to see her again.

But something was clearly wrong since tears still clung to her lashes despite being allowed to come in. As soon as she reached me, I took her arm to pull her into a hug, but her body went stiff and she wavered on her feet. Yes, there was definitely something wrong. I kept my grip on her arm and led her to the nearest velvet couch at the edges of the empty dance floor. The place I first set eyes on her.

"What is it, Reina?" I asked roughly. "You can tell me anything," I said in a softer voice. "Whatever it is, I'll take care of it."

For a split second, she gave me the hint of a smile, but it disappeared just as fast. "I'm pregnant," she blurted, searching my face.

I could read every thought in those eyes, and I didn't doubt for a second that she was telling me the truth or that the baby she carried was mine. I stood, making her choke back a sob, but I wasn't leaving. Instead, I picked her up and whisked her to my office where we could have privacy. She held herself stiffly in my arms, but I held on tight and she finally relaxed a bit against me. I almost didn't want to let her go, but we had much to discuss, so I plopped her down on the couch in my office and shut the door.

"You don't have to worry about a thing, Reina. I'm delighted by this news." I found I wasn't just offering her empty reassurance. I meant it. At forty-four it was well past time I got myself an heir, and here was one attached to a mother I didn't mind the thought of spending the rest of my life with. I didn't mind it at all. "Everything will be fine."

"I don't even know your last name," she said, sitting on the edge of the couch with her hands clasped tightly between her knees.

"That's easy enough to remedy." I held out my hand, trying to tease her back to the confident girl who first caught my eye. "Ivan Morozov. Pleased to meet you."

Her already colorless cheeks went deathly pale. She was nervous before but now she was fearful. So, she'd heard the name, knew what it meant. I shouldn't have been shocked. Anyone who lived in this city for any amount of time and paid attention at all would learn of us. It probably wouldn't have been amiss to be fearful, either.

Finally, she lifted her head and met my eyes with hers again. "Do you… do you do more than just own this club?"

She'd given me honesty, of that I would have bet my life. I knew I had to give her nothing less than the same. "I am the head of the Bratva. The Russian brotherhood."

"The mafia?" she squeaked. But her eyes still stayed firmly on mine. She was brave, I had to give her that.

I nodded. "On top of owning this club, which is completely legitimate, we run various other businesses you may or may not want more information about. I don't allow drugs in this place—"

"But you allow drugs." She raised her chin, which only trembled a little.

"Gambling, security, real estate ventures. My empire is vast, Reina. I'm the king in this city." I sat beside her and took her hand, which lay limp in mine. "And you'll be my queen."

She sat silently, mulling it over, and suddenly gasped, ripping her hand away. "That first night—" She paused, her cheeks flooding with color. Was she remembering the way I pleasured her? Because I was remembering it as she slowly licked her lower lip and turned to me with wide eyes. "I complained about my old coworker—"

"Jimmy Talbot," I said.

"It was you," she wailed. "Did you order that attack?"

"That night I told you to ask for whatever you wanted, and I'd make it happen," I reminded her.

She shook her head hard enough to dislodge the small clip in her hair. She let it hang from her blonde strands as she stared at me. "I never asked for that!"

I slipped the wayward locks behind her ear and placed my hand on her chest, palm over her rapidly beating heart. "I could tell you were asking with this," I said. "I knew what you really wanted." Her breath came quicker, and my hand slowly drifted lower to cup her through her thin top. My own breathing was getting harder to control as she leaned toward me. We were as attracted to each other as that first night, but even more powerfully, if that was possible. "I know what you really want now, Reina. Let me give it to you."

Her eyes closed briefly and I tilted to take her mouth. She jumped up and scurried to the door, yanking it open.

"I can't do this," she said. "I can't handle this. Just let me go."

She turned and slammed out into the hall. I listened to her footsteps getting further away, her sobs tearing me apart. I stayed seated in my office, staring at the doorway. She could think I was letting her go for now. But Reina was mine. She carried my heir. She'd accept the life I had planned, one way or the other.

CHAPTER 7 - REINA

I fled from the club, disgusted with myself for how close I came to crawling into his lap and letting him have his way with me. That was exactly what got me into this predicament in the first place.

Head of a crime syndicate? I only skimmed the headlines every day and even I knew about the Morozov family. After practically running from the club, my legs gave out about ten blocks away. I sat down on a bench, staring at the last of the beach stragglers. The sound of the ocean normally soothed away whatever cares I had, but these current cares refused to be soothed. A storm was brewing far out at sea and it would probably open up on me if I sat there for too long, but I couldn't move.

I shakily searched Ivan's name on my phone, finding article after article. What was true and what was hysterical clickbait? I had no way of knowing, but I read it all.

The Morozov family was both loved and feared depending on who was writing the article, either donating huge, probably dirty, sums of money to art museums or old folk's homes, or else single handedly destroying the fabric of society with gambling rings, prostitution, and owning half the buildings in Miami. There were a few pictures of Ivan, all taken from a distance, or blurry cellphone pics from inside the club. God, he was handsome. God, what was wrong with me?

It didn't seem to matter if the person writing the article was singing the family's praises for whatever massive donation they'd made, everyone seemed to agree they were dangerous. I didn't need to sit out in increasingly rising winds to find that out. I knew it the moment I learned his name. He'd admitted it himself. He'd admitted to having Jimmy beaten.

In a full panic, I got home as fast as I could, blindly throwing clothes into an overnight bag. I needed to get away. But where? A man like Ivan would easily be able to find out where I was from, so going home to Kansas was out. I couldn't risk putting Lynn and Andrew in his path. I scrolled through lists of flights and finally settled on Las Vegas. The ticket was cheap, and it was one of the most anonymous places in the world.

My skin prickled the whole way to the airport, and I was sure they'd pull me for questioning as I went through security since I was acting so jumpy. I only breathed easily once I was on the plane, but then I realized I had no plan, very little money, and only a few changes of clothes.

"That's fine," I muttered, not caring if my seatmate thought I was crazy. I could make a better plan once I was calmer. It hit me that maybe I should get rid of the baby, and just the thought of it made me burst into tears.

"Are you okay?" the passenger next to me asked, looking like he wanted to crawl over me to the emergency exit.

"I'm fine," I said. "I'm just pregnant."

He relaxed and nodded. "Oh, I see. I've got three. My wife gets a little funny with each one, too. Let me know if you need me to get the attendant."

"I don't need anything, thanks," I said, turning to curl up against the window, finally managing to snivel myself to sleep.

Vegas was exactly as it was advertised, full of lights and people who didn't give me a second glance. I found a dinghy little motel far off the main strip and forced myself to pick at the cheap buffet they offered before holing up in my room. I was exhausted despite sleeping on the plane and fell into a fitful sleep on the lumpy bed.

The next morning, I kept my mind blank. There was no use in feeling sorry for myself, and I was most definitely not entertaining the thought of giving up my baby just because its father was a ruthless crime boss.

Was he really so ruthless, though? I drifted into a daydream, recalling the way he'd made my every wish come true the night we spent together.

"And one of those wishes was beating your work rival to a pulp," I said to my haggard reflection in the scuffed bathroom mirror.

Not that I felt sorry for Jimmy, even knowing I inadvertently had something to do with his broken bones. I patted my stomach, never exactly flat, but still no sign I was pregnant. "We need a job, little one," I said.

After I cleaned myself up and did some searching on my phone, I felt quite a bit more optimistic. Sure, I had uprooted my whole life in a matter of twelve hours, but there were tons of bars and restaurants hiring. I could start a new life, no big deal.

Yes, I was faking it a little, but so what? I gripped my old-fashioned motel room key and headed out to pound the pavement. Outside the grimy little cement block building, the bright desert sun hit me like a frying pan, even with being used to the Miami heat. I hurried to walk along the shady side of the motel and wasn't ten feet away when vice-like arms wrapped around my middle and dragged me into an alley. As soon as I screamed, a big, meaty hand clapped over my mouth, cutting it off to a useless yip. I kicked furiously and another big man jumped out and grabbed my legs. Like I was a freshly caught wild hog, they carried me down the alley, thrashing and trying to bite at the sweaty paw across my face.

I should probably have been filled with terror, but I only felt fury, certain of who was behind this. Was Ivan kidnapping me? At the end of the alley, the goon who had my legs dropped them and popped open the trunk of a car parked next to a brick wall.

I slammed my head backward, clipping the chin of the one who held my top half, and dislodged his hand from my mouth.

"No way," I said. "You better not put me in—"

Two seconds later I was up and in the trunk, the top slamming down before I could shout another syllable. I rolled around on the stiff, thinly carpeted surface, kicking at everything I could, thinking about an old safety video from middle school that showed how to dislodge the signal lights and maybe attract the police. There was a slam above me that shocked me into stopping for a moment.

"Knock it off," one of the goons yelled.

"Let me out," I tried. Nothing. "He's going to be pissed you put me in the trunk," I bellowed.

Another slam. "He'll be more pissed if we don't bring you to him, now shut the fuck up. It's not far."

He didn't lie and within minutes the car stopped and the trunk flew open. I was as ready as I could be and tried to leap out. They merely grabbed my arms and shook me.

"We can stuff a bag over your face and carry you up the stairs or you can walk."

I reared my foot back and kicked him in the shin. He barely flinched and the other one dropped my arm and reached into the back seat to pull out a heavy cloth sack.

"I'll walk," I said, recoiling from it.

They both snickered, keeping their hands clamped around my wrists as they frog marched me up some stairs for about three floors, then asked me if I could be trusted to get on the elevator. "It's forty stories," he said, deadpan.

Of course I chose the elevator, surprised to see we were in a swanky hotel when we left the stairwell and entered the wide, richly wallpapered and mirrored hall. I was being kidnapped in plain sight, but I didn't doubt they would follow through and put the bag over my head if I made a scene. I didn't doubt that Ivan had some sway at this place and that no one would lift a finger to help me, either.

They finally pushed me through the door of a vast suite and slammed it shut behind me. And there he was, smugly sitting on a brocade armchair in front of a sweeping view of the Vegas strip, as golden and beautiful as ever. Just like the king he was. As pissed as I was, and despite the fear that started to simmer, I felt a rush of lust as I took him in. My legs betrayed me and took a step closer to him. His lips curled in a taunting smile.

"I can't believe you did this," I said.

"Can't you?" was his only reply. "Did you think it would be more than a minor inconvenience to me, you running off to Vegas like this?" He shrugged, his smile growing wider. "I really should thank you since you actually ended up making things easier in the long run."

"What do you mean?" I asked. He looked way too pleased with himself.

"I mean, we're going to be married, Reina."

My stomach dipped at the same time that troublesome lust surged. "Like hell we are. I'm going to walk out of here, and if you don't let me, there will be a scene, and it'll be so big, not even all the people you've bought off will be able to ignore it."

He stood from his throne, sidling over to me, his big body looming over mine, and still he had that smug look of ownership on his face. The one that claimed he owned *me*, the one that was destroying my panties. He calmly handed me his phone.

"I don't think you will," he said.

Confused, I looked at his phone, my heart constricting. The slight fear that had been at the edges of my consciousness raced to the forefront. On his screen were pictures of my best friends. Lynn in line at the grocery store, outside of her house. Andrew loading up one of his company trucks. Dozens more pictures of them.

"Those two are very important to you, aren't they?" he asked. "It would be a shame if anything happened to them."

Everything went ten shades of red, and I flew at him, scratching at whatever my hands could reach. He pinned my arms to my sides and pressed me against the wall, his face so close I had to close my eyes to keep from melting into his heated gaze. His lips grazed my cheek as he yanked my hands over my head, gripping my wrists together while his free hand roamed down my body. My nipples rose to greet him as he stroked my breasts, and I couldn't help the soft moan that escaped my mouth.

"I hate you," I cried, wanting to sound like a snarling wolf but only sounding like a bleating lamb.

His hand continued slowly down my body to rest on my stomach. "I don't believe you," he said. "Open your eyes and look at me, Reina." I did as he commanded, instantly lost in his deep blue eyes. Damn him. My chest heaved as he splayed his fingers across my belly. "This child is mine, and so are you."

When he pulled his hand away, for a split second, I was bereft, but he still held my hands tight above my head. He pulled a ring out of his pocket and forced it on my finger, then kissed my palm. I wanted to slap him, but the feel of his lips made me weak, more helpless than before he let go of me.

"We're engaged now," he said, his hand back on my breast, kneading, coaxing. "Don't you want to enjoy this happy moment?"

He pulled me close to him, so I felt every inch of his hard desire against me. His mouth claimed mine, urging my lips to part for his questing tongue. The unquenchable lust that made me hate myself more than I hated him devoured me. I writhed against him, no longer wanting to fight that dark part of me that only wanted what he was offering—no, demanding.

"Yes," I sobbed furiously, digging my fingertips into his muscular, unyielding chest. "I want to enjoy it." I kept digging, then pushing, letting my head drop back as he held me close and slipped his hand between my thighs, fully awakening my insatiable need for him. "I want you inside me right now, hard and fast. Make me yours like you seem to think I am."

He leaned back, momentarily stunned by my harsh words. I grabbed at the thick bulge pulsing through his pants. It only took me a second to get his cock free and I nearly cried with relief when it was in my hand. His hand covered mine to ease my fevered grip, then he sighed as I pumped him up and down, unable to take my eyes from his throbbing member.

With a low growl, he picked me up and slammed me against the wall, yanking down my jeans and panties with one swift motion. "Hold onto me, my queen," he ordered, and I wrapped my legs around his waist.

He was deep inside me only a second later, pinning me to the wall like I'd been impaled. But it was oh-so-sweet, and exactly what I'd been craving since I'd been shoved into that room. He did as I begged, taking me hard and fast, his face buried in my hair. With every thrust, I got closer to the edge, holding on to him tighter. He found my clit while still holding me up and, as his fingers stroked me, I leaned back my head and screamed. He laughed as he gave one final thrust, which soon turned into a roar.

He staggered back with me in his arms, landing on his big brocade throne. Pulling me close, he tugged back my hair and kissed me deeply.

"My queen," he murmured, still catching his breath.

"I hate you," I answered, dropping my face to his chest and closing my eyes as his laughter rumbled up against my cheek.

CHAPTER 8 - IVAN

My blushing bride was stewing by herself on my private jet back to Miami. I didn't mind, knowing I could raise her passion whenever I chose. We'd enjoyed a very nice but far too short honeymoon in my suite in Vegas, after our quickie wedding in one of the tacky chapels on the strip. Once she settled into her new life, perhaps I'd see if she wanted a better ceremony, maybe a reception afterwards. I couldn't keep my eyes off her as she pretended to read the book she bought at the airport, the only thing she'd accept from me.

I was unaccountably fond of her and wanted to shower her with lavish gifts and attention, but once we were back home, I had to keep that under wraps. No one could know she meant so much to me, not with things being so tense with the Balakins. Even without that, the only people I truly trusted in my organization were my brothers. Anyone could turn on me at any time for the right price and up until now, there was no one special enough to me that an enemy could use against me. My brothers could hold their own, but I'd have sooner died than put Reina and my heir in danger.

She pouted the whole drive back to my mansion, and I was gratified to see her finally stop scowling when she saw the place.

"What happened to that apartment?" she asked, staring in awe at the huge house on the waterway.

"That's only one of my properties. This is another, and the place where you'll stay," I explained.

Her eyebrows shot up. "You're not staying here, too?"

I laughed at getting her to admit she cared, at least a little bit. She quickly went back to giving me the silent treatment after I assured her I would be living with her. No matter how much she said she despised me, her body said otherwise and she'd eagerly enjoyed every night of our honeymoon in Vegas. I might not be able to show how much I liked my little queen when others were around, but I could certainly show her in our private time together.

It pained me when the staff flung open the doors to greet us. I moved away from her, my demeanor going icy the way they expected, but was a shock to Reina. "Get her settled in the west suite," I snapped, shoving her toward the wide, curving staircase.

She'd been blinking up at the crystal chandelier in the airy entrance hall, but now she blinked at me, confused by my sudden change. The hurt in her eyes pained me, but I pretended she didn't exist once I gave my orders regarding where she was to stay, then marched to my office. I didn't look back to make sure she was going up the stairs. I could count on my staff to see her to her suite. I had work to do, and it was safer if people assumed she was little more than a house guest, and one that wasn't quite welcome at that.

I forgot my discomfort and the urge to race up the stairs after her when I saw my brothers waiting for me in my office. Not just Aleksei but Nicolai and Yuri as well. Things must have escalated in the three days I was gone. My fury grew as Aleksei filled me in on the newest encroachment on our territory, still intimidating the businesses that rented my many buildings.

"Don't they understand you literally own those properties?" hotheaded Nicolai ranted. He proposed we storm the small hotel where the head of the Balakins operated, but Aleksei shot him down, still wanting us to somehow magically all work together peacefully. Yuri, who was a tax lawyer and only part of our business dealings because he shared our name, sighed and surprisingly agreed with Nicolai.

We all gaped at him. The youngest, he was the one who kept us off the government's radar by cleaning up our records and making sure our taxes passed muster. He never got his hands dirty and normally came down more on the diplomacy side of things when we were divided. I was the deciding vote, always, and could toss all their opinions if I wanted.

"You want to gun down a bunch of old people at the Rosewell Hotel?" Aleksei asked, voice dripping with disdain.

I side eyed him. I would have wondered if he was really a Morozov if I hadn't seen his ruthless side myself in the past. I couldn't say he'd grown soft, far from it, but the last few years he'd been advocating more and more for peace. And we'd had a few very peaceful years, until the Balakins moved in and ruined it.

"What I want is to put a stop to this," Yuri said. "They're making messes we can't clean up fast enough. We work hard to keep our business out of view, and that makes it easier to keep the right people in the right frame of mind."

"What have you heard?" I asked. "Are we having trouble with our contacts in law enforcement? The city government?" If normal people knew how much low-down gangsters like me relied on local lawmakers they'd be shocked. If they knew how corrupt many people in their government really were, they'd cry themselves to sleep at night.

Yuri threw up his hands. "Not yet, but I can see them getting antsy if crimes keep getting connected to Russian families. No one will take the time to sort who is who, and since we're the biggest, we'll take the fall. Count on it."

"We crush them, then," Nicolai said.

Aleksei jumped in. "We're not crushing anyone. Listen, Ivan. Trust me on this. I've made an appointment to meet Sergey Balakin, their leader. I think he's as fed up as we are with his son making stupid calls. He'll bring him to heel with the right incentives."

I sat back and listened to them arguing amongst themselves until Aleksei clapped his hands loudly to get my attention. I cleared my throat and tried to pretend I hadn't drifted away to my honeymoon.

"Get your head in the game, brother," he said. "Is that woman going to be a problem?"

I stood up and grabbed his collar before he knew what was happening. I tightened my grip until he lowered his gaze. "My head is always in the game," I told him coldly. "And that woman is now your sister-in-law, so keep a respectful tone when you speak of her."

I dropped his shirt and he broke into a grin, turning to the others. "I told you," he said triumphantly. "I knew you didn't just go to Vegas for no reason."

The three of them congratulated me heartily enough to make me blush at the brotherly affection. Then they grew serious, exchanging another look.

"But why the haste?" Nicolai asked. "You haven't known her long."

"You should have had me draw up a prenup," Yuri said.

"She's pregnant with my heir," I said, putting a stop to their nonsense. "The baby will own everything one day, and we won't be getting divorced, so there was no need for a prenup."

As excited as they were to hear about the new addition to the family, I swore them to secrecy. They understood at once how vital it was to Reina's safety that no one knew how important she was.

I told them we'd go ahead with the meeting with Sergey Balakin to see if he could get his son under control and hopefully avoid a war between our families. I had more at stake than I ever had before.

Since I'd been gone for several days, I had to check in with the club, so I ordered my best guard to keep an eye on Reina. She wasn't to leave the house without me, and if she wanted to walk in the garden, he was to stay with her at all times. I decided not to go upstairs and explain it to her, wanting to avoid her ire. My queen was going to hate what she'd see as imprisonment, but it was for her own good. As much as I loved her spirit, too much bravery could get her in trouble and the thought of anything happening to her or the baby was untenable to me.

She would learn to deal with it, and I'd make it up to her that night in bed.

Chapter 9 - Reina

I sat on my private balcony, staring out at the waterway, keeping track of one of the boats that passed by for the umpteenth time in the three weeks since I'd been trapped there. I would have killed someone to be on that sailboat. Or out in the garden. Or at freaking Taco Bell, just to get out of the house for a while. I'd had a doctor visit me and give me a thorough exam. She announced everything was fine and gave me vitamins. I got delicious, nutritious meals whenever I was hungry and had two manicures and two pedicures, plus three full body massages and a haircut by a top stylist.

I was surrounded by books, new clothes, jewelry, shoes, and makeup palettes in my luxurious suite. Ivan's goon Maksim, who seemed to hate his job of guarding me as much as I hated him having to do it, showed up every day with a new card or board game in an attempt to keep me from ripping my newly styled hair out. I had a computer but all social media and email was locked down on it, and I quickly grew tired of YouTube videos. I was only allowed an hour of phone time every day. I only got that because I assured Ivan that my friends, whose lives I still worried were in danger if I made an attempt to climb over the balcony and pull a runner, would tear Miami apart looking for me if I suddenly stopped communicating with them. And the phone call was monitored by either Maksim or my maid, Hetty, who was a sweetheart, but still no better than a jailer as far as I was concerned.

In short, I was kind of miserable. I couldn't say unequivocally miserable because Ivan didn't completely ignore me. He visited most nights, and no matter how hard I tried to resist him, he was simply irresistible. Not just in bed, which was over-the-top amazing and the only time I wasn't ready to swing a leg over the side of the balcony, but he often ate dinner with me, sharing his day and then raptly listening to me mostly complain. He rubbed my feet, gave me head massages that rivaled the masterful way he had with his tongue. *Oh boy, the things he could do with his tongue.*

It didn't make sense why he was so downright mean to me whenever anyone else was around. Even in front of Maksim and Hetty, he'd be brusque or completely ignore me. I didn't understand it, and it hurt more than I wanted to admit to myself. Was he ashamed of me? Wish he'd knocked up someone else?

As I watched the boat on the waterway and contemplated the distance from the balcony to the patio below and my chances of making it across the vast back garden and over the high fence before Maksim tackled me, I tried not to think about the way Ivan had snapped at me the night before. The only people around were his regular goons and some of the house staff, and they'd all looked down, embarrassed for me to be treated like dirt by my husband. Sometimes I wasn't even convinced they knew we were married.

Then only an hour later, he came into my suite with a rose he'd picked from the garden and a shower of kisses. Of course I threw the rose at him and shut myself in the bathroom to keep from responding to the kisses, but he managed to make me forgive him again when he gave me some baloney about wanting to protect me. The truth of the matter was, I needed to feel his touch. He was like an addiction to me and the cravings throughout the day were bad. There was no way I could hold out for too long when he did spend time with me.

"Miss Reina?" Hetty poked her head out, phone in hand.

It was my allotted time to speak with the outside world and I jumped up, following her into my sitting area. Maksim lounged at my desk, pretending to be engrossed in a game of solitaire, but I knew he'd be hanging on every word.

As soon as I heard Lynn's voice, and she assured me that she, the baby, and Andrew were all fine, I was able to relax and settle in for a good long chat. Or at least until my hour was up.

"How's the new job going?" she asked.

About a week before I made up a fake new job at Ivan's club because it was getting too unbelievable to think I could go that long on my meager savings. "It's fine." I wanted to get onto another subject because I hated lying to her.

"And how are things with Ivan?"

Her voice took on a singsong quality because supposedly I'd been taking things slow with my new boss. Yes, more lies. But there was no way I could explain my real situation. I wouldn't be able to sell that we were happily married, and if I was that good at deception, she would have been hurt not to be invited to the wedding.

"Great," I said, trying not to choke on the words. "We're, uh, still taking things slow and getting to know each other."

I could practically hear Maksim's eyes rolling from across the room. I tried to play off a dinner in my room as a romantic night out at a restaurant to make it seem like Ivan and I were dating. Not a word about how he was cold as ice when we weren't alone or how I'd become obsessed with peering over my balcony.

Not a peep about how much I hate him but also can't keep my hands off him. As happy as I was to get to talk to Lynn, I hated thinking about my relationship with Ivan. I knew he was excited about having an heir, but I wasn't convinced he was happy. Not with me, anyway. I couldn't help but wonder as I watched the boats go by, what was going to become of me once the baby was born. I sniffled and quickly tried to hide it.

"What's wrong?" she asked, catching the sound of my misery.

"Nothing," I said quickly, with a glance at Maksim. "Just hormone craziness. You know."

That got her off the trail and we spent most of my time talking about our symptoms, doctor updates, and the curtains she and Andrew picked for the nursery.

I got all morose again since it would have been laughable trying to get Ivan to help me pick baby decor. Laughable if it weren't so sad.

"I ran into Detective Sosa at the pharmacy," she said after we switched subjects. "I wasn't sure I should say anything, but he did ask how you were."

I counted to ten to keep from taking the flash of anger out on Lynn. "I hope you told him I'd be better if he solved my dad's case," I said.

She sighed. "I'm really sorry, hon, but there wasn't anything new. He keeps hitting dead ends."

I didn't have anything to say to that except rude epithets, so I kept my teeth ground together. Maksim stood up and made a big show of pointing to his watch. It was just as well the hour was nearly up because thinking about my dad's case still being unsolved put my already sour mood right over the edge. I made a dumb excuse to end the call and chucked the phone at Maksim.

"There's no one else I want to call," I snapped.

I should have called Detective Sosa and harangued him about the so-called dead ends, but I knew I'd just end up in a puddle of frustrated tears. I looked back and forth between Hetty and Maksim, sick to death of my keepers. I barreled past Hetty and swerved around my husband's head goon.

"Run and tattle to your master if you want, but I'm going outside and you better keep your distance if you're going to follow me."

Shockingly, I made it downstairs with no one on my tail, and stormed through the kitchen and out the back door. The garden was gorgeous, and I meant to see more of it than just the small area where I'd had a few dinners with Ivan and the view from my balcony. I started toward the left perimeter and followed the high stone wall, trying to get my heart to stop hurting. According to the doctor, it was important to stay calm, but I would have loved for her to explain how I was supposed to do that. Of course she'd never feel sorry for me, since she had to be on Ivan's payroll.

I kept trying to tell myself that my beloved father didn't need justice to be able to rest in peace. He was a good, honest, hard-working man so there was no reason he wasn't happy where he was. But I wasn't happy. I wasn't at peace. The bastard who'd stolen him from me needed to rot in prison for his crime.

By the time I made it to the back corner, I felt a tiny bit better from being surrounded by all the heavy green foliage. The part of the garden closest to the mansion was well-manicured with exotic, tropical flowers that parakeets and lovebirds fluttered around. There were white, crushed shell paths and fountains with benches around them. Back here by the edges, it was wild and I could imagine I was free in the jungle, anywhere but where I really was. I stood on my toes and saw a bamboo roof sticking up above the palm fronds and headed toward it.

It turned out to be a small, windowless shed, but the corrugated metal door was open a crack, and I thought I heard voices. Getting a little closer, I definitely heard a man saying something in a harsh growl I would have recognized anywhere. But why was Ivan way out here in this dark little shed?

Something warned me to turn around and pretend I never found that spot, and the closer I crept to the open doorway, the more urgent that something tried to get me to stop. But I was in a bad, stubborn mood still and curiosity made me keep going. At the doorway, I peeked around the rusty metal edge. The single room shed was almost too dark to see anything, especially being out in the blazing Florida sun. I could hear fine, though, and the noises coming from the shed curdled my blood.

"Tell us what you know or suffer the consequences," Ivan said from the shadowy depths. It sounded like he was just on the other side of the door.

From deeper inside the shed I heard a low groan and a weak voice muttered something I couldn't make out.

"So you refuse," Ivan said. Another groan. "Go ahead," Ivan ordered.

There was the distinct noise of a fist hitting flesh and the groan intensified. Once again Ivan demanded for the person to tell what he knew. Once again he refused and the smack sounded again. My heart raced as I realized someone was being tortured on the very property where I now lived. I leaned closer, my fingernails cutting into my palms as my hands tightened into fists. This was exactly what the man who killed my father deserved. I should have been horrified, but all I felt was grim satisfaction. I leaned closer, holding my breath as Ivan asked the man to confess, warning that this was his final chance.

Then a loud cracking noise and a guttural scream that made me jump back an entire foot. The rotting wood base around the shed crumbled under my heel and I teetered backwards, grabbing the door by reflex to keep from falling on my ass. It flew open as I stumbled, and I saw a man I didn't recognize raising a bloody bat over another man tied to a folding chair. If his pulp of a face and blood-soaked shirt was any indication, this wasn't the first blow he'd received. His entire front was a wash of red, his arms razored with cuts. I glimpsed a small table full of knives and dear God, *saws.* The blades of some of them were already stained. Ivan stood with his arms crossed and his legs wide, surveying the carnage. If I had one wish right then I wouldn't have used it to gain my freedom. I would have made myself disappear when Ivan turned and saw me.

His brow furrowed as he stepped toward me, blue eyes shooting daggers. I tried to explain I wasn't spying, lie that I hadn't seen anything so his rage wouldn't be turned on me. Instead, I turned and ran like hell back toward the house.

Chapter 10 - Ivan

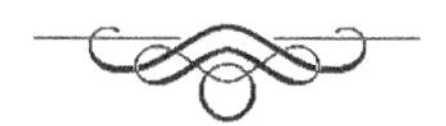

I was furious that she saw what I'd been doing, but more furious at myself when I saw the fear in her eyes thinking my anger was directed at her. I scowled at the man who would rather die than admit he'd lied and betrayed me, then told my cousin to keep working while I ran after her.

By the time I caught up to her, Maksim had already grabbed her. She fought him valiantly, kicking and swearing, as he led her back toward the house. I had to force down a tender smile at her wild display and hide my pride in her lioness' heart. I roughly took her arm and shook her.

"How dare you defy my orders? You'll pay for this dearly."

She immediately stopped thrashing and shrunk into herself, as I dragged her up the stairs to her room. I hated every minute of my act, but loudly berated her all the same.

"You're not to go to that part of the estate again," I said. "Why weren't you with Maksim? Does he need to be punished because of your foolishness and stubbornness and inability to follow my rules?"

Her eyes sparkled with tears that she angrily blinked away when we were finally alone in her room. Slamming the door behind me to complete the charade, I leaned against it and sighed.

"Damn it, Reina. Why did you disobey me like that?" My tone was much softer now, but I couldn't hide my frustration.

Wandering the property alone like that made my stomach turn with worry for her safety. I hated my strict rules as much as she did, but she didn't—*couldn't* understand the kind of people who were at the perimeters of my life. Even the people closest to me might snap and turn on me at any time, striking out at the thing that would hurt me the most. I moved closer to her and tried to smooth her bedraggled hair, which had come free from its ponytail after her run and tussle with Maksim.

She jerked away from me, shaking her head. "Were you going to kill that man?" she asked.

She wouldn't like it, but as always, she'd only get the truth from me. "That man should already be dead, Reina, and believe me, nothing of value will be lost."

I braced myself for her disgust or fear, but before I could explain what the man did to deserve his fate, I saw that she looked almost satisfied.

"Why?" Her eyes gleamed as she crossed her arms over her chest.

"Why is he dead or why did I have him killed?" I asked, locking eyes with her. I smiled when my brave queen refused to look away.

"How about both."

I nodded. "He kidnapped a girl who worked for me. I'm not a saint, Reina. Probably not even a good man. But I have certain standards. Don't take what's mine, don't lie to me about it. He did both those things and hurt someone who didn't deserve to be hurt on top of it. I hurt people, make no mistake. But I try to be sure they deserve it."

"Good," she whispered. "I'm glad you did it, then."

I was so turned on by her, I stepped forward and cupped her face in my hands, desperate for her to really see me and want me as badly as I wanted her. "If ever I'm in the same position as the man you saw in the shed, I'll probably deserve it, too. Will you mourn me, Reina?"

For a moment, she went pale, and I had the fleeting hope she cared for me at least a little, then she shook her head, and it felt like my heart stopped beating. A slow smile took over her pretty face. "You won't ever be in that position," she said. "Because you won't ever deserve it." She pushed my hands away and reached for my shirt, yanking me close. "Promise me you only kill bad people." She shook her head. Was she remembering I was one of those bad people? "Promise me you've never killed someone innocent, someone who's not a part of your business."

"I promise. I swear it."

She stood on her toes and kissed me. I reached for her and pulled her flush with my body. After our tongues tangled wildly for a moment, she shoved me away and sank onto the bed, putting her head in her hands.

I sat beside her and put my arm around her, gratified when she didn't push me away. I had to remember that no matter that she was as fierce as a lioness, she'd just seen something pretty gruesome and had to face the fact that her husband was a killer.

"I'm so sorry, my little queen," I said, stroking her back. "This stress can't be good for the baby."

She shot me a dark look. "Being locked up all the time can't be either. I'm sick to death of this pampered prison. That's why I ran away from your guard and Hetty in the first place. I just needed some time away from this room." She slapped the covers. "Anything, even a trip through the drive-thru would seem like heaven if I could just get out for a while."

"I'll think of something," I promised. "And it will be better than fast food, I swear."

Chapter 11 - Reina

The next few days passed without any sign of Ivan, so I knew he must have been out of town. Whenever he was here he always spent time with me. I might not have known how he felt about me where his heart was concerned, but his other parts liked me just fine. We always had a civilized dinner together, then one of us wouldn't be able to hold out anymore, and pounce. He never stayed the entire night with me. No matter if our arms and legs were intertwined when I fell asleep, he was always gone when I woke up in the morning.

It left me feeling a little bit dirty, but also somewhat relieved to have space to myself after our fervent interludes. Whenever he was near me he seemed to take up all the oxygen in the room, and definitely all my attention.

How did he do it? Every day I schooled myself to resist him, feeling like he had too much power over me. It would last until Hetty laid out the evening's pretty dress for me and helped me do my hair and makeup. It was like getting ready for a date, but it wasn't a suitor trying to impress me, it was my husband and we never left the house. When I heard his gruff voice outside my door sending Maksim away, my resolve began to crumble. Just the sound of his low, rumbling voice sent anticipation coursing through my veins. As soon as he walked through my door, it was all over. There was no fighting, because I didn't want to fight. I only wanted to feel his strong arms around me, and his lips on mine. And so much more. Ivan wasn't stingy with gifts, and he was even more generous with his body.

Then I woke up alone, and it started all over again. The self-recrimination, the resolve, the throwing myself at him the second he smiled at me. If I wasn't so sure I hated him, I would have started to think I was falling in love with my husband.

As usual, I sat on my balcony, flipping through one of the stacks of magazines Hetty brought me every day. This one was from France, featuring the scandals of their own celebrities, and I couldn't understand a word, just looked at the glossy pictures to pass the endless time. Trying not to think about Ivan, but craving him desperately since it had been three days without seeing him. It pissed me off, and I tossed the magazine to grab one that I could understand so I could stop obsessing about when I'd see him again. When I could feel his expert touch.

Hetty stuck her head out and told me there was a new delivery.

Whoop-de-doo. She looked so excited and was so kind to me that I pretended as best I could to give a crap and followed her inside. The big, cream leather couch was loaded down with garment bags and there were stacks of shoe boxes lined up next to it. The entire surface of the big glass coffee table was hidden under smaller boxes, some flat and long, some square, some tiny with perfect little bows on them.

Even my grumpy heart picked up at the sight of such bounty. "Where should we start?" I asked Hetty.

She began to unzip all the garment bags while I tore into the shoeboxes, squealing at each pair. It was shoe lover's Christmas, and my mood brightened as I tried them on. Hetty held up each sumptuous gown, and I grabbed the shoes I thought would look best with them and soon we had six stunning outfits hanging from the bar and draped across the couch.

"This must mean it's your date night tonight," Hetty said, motioning toward the smaller boxes. "You know what those must be."

"Accessories," I breathed, fully taken by the sweet surprise.

This was almost as good as shopping. It was insane how I would have picked every one of the dresses myself, and certainly all of the shoes, if I could have afforded them. How did he know me so well?

Sure enough, there were three designer clutches along with a treasure trove of jewelry in all those other boxes. My eyes ached from the amount of sparkle and shine, and I finally leaned against the couch from my spot on the floor with at least a hundred thousand dollars' worth of bling strewn across my lap. Hetty opened the last box to reveal an actual diamond and emerald tiara and we both cracked up laughing after I reached for it and popped it on her head.

She hurriedly took it off and nestled it back in its satin box, shaking her head. "Do you know what time you should be ready?"

I slumped, because of course I didn't. Ivan didn't consult with me, he ordered me around. Or his goons did. I got up and scurried to the door, startling Maksim, who gave me his customary dirty look.

"Ask your boss what time I'm supposed to be ready, if I'm supposed to be ready at all," I said bitterly.

He tapped out a message on his phone and glared at me while he waited for a reply. I glared right back. His phone pinged a few seconds later and he told me seven o'clock. Hetty sucked in a breath behind me.

"It's four-thirty now. We have to get started."

Slamming the door on Maksim, I turned around and looked at my living area, which now resembled Aladdin's cave with all the riches. Truth be told I was tired of being miserable, either angry or resentful or just plain sad. My intense morning sickness had mostly subsided and apparently I was about to get a night out on the town. I wanted to let go and have some fun.

Hetty was as good of a friend as I had in that situation, and she was just as eager to get me glammed up as I was to look amazing. She wanted me to choose the full-length, green silk gown and to wear the tiara with it, describing how she wanted to put my hair up.

"It's not prom, Hetty, it's just a date." But my cheeks grew warm, and I couldn't hide my smile thinking about it. Not just getting to leave the house, but spending time with Ivan. I wanted him to find me attractive.

"He wouldn't have picked this dress if he didn't want you to wear it," she said. "And it fits you like a glove."

I had tried it on just to get her to stop nagging me, and it really did look perfect. My stomach barely pooched out and the supple fabric skimmed the rest of my curves, accenting them in all the best places. When I walked across the room and did a dramatic turn like I was in a runway show, the silk swished enticingly along my calves.

"Fine, I'll wear it."

How could I not? This was my big night out. It had been just under a month since my "wedding," if the tense ceremony in the neon chapel in Vegas counted as one, and this was the first time I was getting to leave the secluded grounds. Hetty cheered and then made me get out of it so she could fix my hair and makeup. By the time she was done, I almost thought I could go down to any agency on the beach and get signed. If I was six inches taller, anyway.

"You're a miracle worker," I told her, twisting and turning to admire my new look.

"Eh, you're very pretty, Miss Reina. Just accept it."

I wished she wouldn't call me Miss. It only reminded me we weren't really two friends hanging out. I refused to let it dampen my excitement while we picked out what jewelry and bag I would use. I flatly refused to wear the tiara. That was just too much. In the end, I chose a delicate, emerald-encrusted bracelet and diamond drop earrings. We decided against any of the necklaces to make my ample cleavage the star of the show.

"This is ridiculous," I said, anxiously twisting the bracelet. It had to be worth more than a car. "Who wears jewelry like this?"

"People who live in houses like this," Hetty said with a shrug. "People like you, Miss Reina."

There was a sharp rap at the door, and Ivan came through it. I barely noticed Hetty skittering around him to leave because he took my breath away. Dressed in a crisp and perfectly tailored, dark gray suit with a snowy white shirt he looked even taller than usual. He was clean-shaven and while I loved the feel of his rough stubble against my tender skin, his strong jaw and full lips not being hidden made me realize just exactly how handsome he was. Even the intense look in his eyes was softened a little by his smooth cheeks and it made him a bit less intimidating. Only a bit, because his eyes were as fierce as always as he looked me up and down. There was ownership in his gaze, which made me bristle even as it sent shivers all over my skin. There was also pride there, which made me puff up and extra grateful for Hetty's help.

"You constantly surprise me with your beauty, Reina," he said, sweeping me into his arms.

I melted against him and smoothed his tie, shades of blue and green that made his stormy eyes pop. My stubbornness wouldn't let me thank him for all the clothes and jewelry, but I refused to let it ruin our night. Standing on my toes, even in my sky high heels, I kissed him.

"Where are we going?" I pulled away before things got heated. Yes, I wanted him, but I needed this night of freedom.

"Wherever you desire, my queen." He tapped me on the nose and spun on his heel.

I followed him down the stairs, knowing better than to expect him to offer me his hand or put his arm around me when anyone else was around. Outside, a sleek, silver convertible waited in the circular drive by the front doors.

"Get in," he grunted after he opened the passenger side door.

Small favors, I supposed, sliding onto the leather seat. He slammed the door, almost getting the hem of my gown before I could swing it in after me, and hurried to take the driver's seat. I wasn't sure if I was glad he was driving or sorry, because despite his rude treatment, I was already in agony to touch him again. I thought about our first meeting when I drunkenly climbed in his lap in the back of his car and looked at my hands to hide my blush.

The convertible squealed away from the mansion when he floored the gas without a word or a glance to see if I had my seatbelt on. He only turned to me once we were on the main road at the end of the long driveway.

I huffed, hating the way my heart constricted at his smile. "Why are you only nice to me when we're alone?"

The smile faded. "I've told you. You mustn't question me about these things."

Blah blah blah, my safety, whatever. The sight of the palm trees lining the roads soon turning into shops and restaurants made me drop it, not wanting to spoil my night of freedom. Plus, when I turned to him to argue, his chiseled profile stopped me in my tracks and I reached to draw my finger down his smooth jaw. His smile came back and I knew I'd made the right choice.

"Tell me what you want to do," he said. "Anything. I'll make it happen."

"What if I said I wanted to go to Paris, but I don't have a passport?" I asked. All those French magazines made me yearn to travel, but I had never left the US in all my twenty-three years.

"Simple," he said. "Shall I call my pilot?"

I believed him, but I got a sudden craving that almost made me double over when we passed a fried chicken restaurant and the smell wafted over us. I laughed, twisting to look back at the chicken shack.

"I was just joking before about going through the drive through, but now I'm actually really hungry for some of that chicken."

He did a u-turn in the middle of the street, earning a few angry honks. He repeated everything I asked for into the speaker and when they handed over the buckets, I asked if we could eat it on the beach.

"Anything you want," he said magnanimously. "You're making things too simple."

"I'll make you jump through hoops later," I promised, running my hand up his thigh.

He turned to me with a raised eyebrow and a wicked look that almost made me forget the chicken. "Don't tempt me to take you back home right now." He must have seen my disappointment because he leaned over to kiss me quickly. "Don't worry. I can wait."

His husky voice and the feel of his lips brushing mine made me wonder if I cared so much about this night of freedom after all. But as he turned onto the main strand and the ocean crashing mingled with the sounds of happy people settling in for their own date nights, I wanted to be part of it.

I slipped off my shoes as soon as we got off the sidewalk, grinning at the decadent feeling of sand between my toes while wearing a designer evening gown. We took the food out onto the beach and he pulled off his jacket for me to sit on, plunking down in the sand in his expensive trousers as if he had cut-offs on instead. I scarfed down the crispy chicken and all the sides like I was eating for an entire family, not just one extra person, and caught him looking at me with pride while my cheeks were full of coleslaw.

"Prize porker, huh?" I joked, but his eyebrows shot together in a scowl.

"You're nourishing our child," he said. "And taking care of this body I love so much."

He wrapped his arm around me and squeezed. I was stunned and heat coursed through me, not just at his touch but his words. It was the first time he'd called the baby our child and not just his heir and the way he'd said the word love, even though it was just in reference to my body, shook me to my core. But in a good way or a bad way? I had no idea. Ivan was great at confusing me, that was one thing that was certain.

The sun was down and the ocean was just a dark, whooshing mass in front of us, but the lights from the hotels behind us were bright enough that we could take a walk along the sand.

"We can't just leave the trash," I said, more outraged at this crime than I had ever felt about his mob business.

He rolled his eyes at me and pulled me down the beach. A glance back showed a couple of his men picking up the food containers and carrying them away. I sighed. Of course we wouldn't really be alone.

"Are they for safety or just cleanup?" I asked.

He leaned down and kissed me. "Shush, my queen. You're too beautiful tonight to worry."

There was no use in arguing when he took that final tone, so I leaned against him as we strolled down the beach. We passed a few other couples and got some looks due to my outrageous dress, but since it was Miami, no one gave us much attention. Pretty soon we were on a secluded stretch and Ivan tugged me toward an empty lifeguard station.

"Shall we sit and enjoy the sounds of the surf for a while?" he asked, his hand moving from my waist to my hip.

I licked my lips and nodded as he led me behind the tower. I laughed when I saw what waited there, and shouldn't have been surprised because it was Ivan, but I was. He pulled me down beside him on the thick blanket, and took the champagne bottle out of the ice bucket sitting at the edge. There was also a tray of strawberries and mango slices, both my favorites.

"How did you do this?" I asked. "We didn't plan to come here."

"My men are good for more than just security and trash cleanup," he said with a smirk. He held up his phone. "Whenever you looked away. I could have been messaging my mistress for all you noticed."

The idea of that sent a wash of fury over me and I guess it showed on my face because he threw back his head and laughed. Holding out a strawberry, he pressed it against my pursed lips.

"You're the only woman in my life, Reina. You're my queen, remember? Now, open that pretty mouth for me."

My lips parted to accept the strawberry as satisfaction replaced my sudden anger. "As long as you know it," I said, snapping my teeth down on the juicy berry. "You may be the king of the Bratva around here and I'm just a nobody from Kansas, but I'll find a way to make you pay if you ever share this with anyone else again."

I kept his gaze as I slid my hand up his thigh to press against the thick bulge that rose with my touch. My satisfaction grew at this small bit of power I had over Ivan and leaned closer.

"Never," he said, his lips crashing against mine.

We were rolling on the blanket, grappling each other and making out like teenagers when we heard shouts of laughter coming from up the beach. I tapped his shoulder and sat up.

"We should act civilized," I said, patting my swollen lips and trying to cool down.

Ivan stared at the group of young men walking along the shore, his jaw tensing. As they got closer I could hear snippets of their loud talk and I recognized the accent. I was around it constantly now. These men were Russian as sure as Ivan was growing more agitated.

I edged closer to him and he calmly reached for the champagne bottle, but made no move to pour us any. "It's fine, Reina," he said.

Well, considering I hadn't asked, I decided it wasn't fine. "We should go," I said. "We can cut through the hotel and walk on the street to get back to the car."

He shook his head, his eyes never leaving the group. *Let them pass by.* This was our night. As they drew parallel with us, I decided there was no way they could even see us, far up the sand and half hidden in the shadows of the lifeguard stand. I was wrong, and they turned to head toward us.

Ivan jumped up, whisking me behind him, one hand wrapped around the neck of the champagne bottle, the other working his phone. I looked around for his goons, the one and only time I would have been glad to see them, but it was only darkness all the way to the hotel far up on the other side of the strand.

The group reached us and stopped, staring at Ivan, who stared back. There were five of them, all dressed in jeans and t-shirts, and young. Maybe even younger than me. One of them stood ahead of the small pack, his chin jutting forward and a sneer on his face.

"Don't you have a home, Ivan Morozov?" His accent was much heavier than Ivan's almost imperceptible one. "You have to fuck your whores outside like the dog you are?"

Oh no. I almost felt sorry for the kid. Almost. Ivan shook his head.

"You're making a mistake, Anton," he said, his voice so icy I hugged my arms close to my chest. "You shouldn't be embarrassing your father like this."

The other guys looked at each other and shuffled back a little. They seemed to have some smarts, or self-preservation at least. Anton, their clear leader, didn't. He leaned forward, his face a stony mask of hatred.

"I think my father would be proud of me for taking the initiative," he spat. I didn't like the sound of that. I didn't like it at all when Ivan remained silent as Anton laughed bitterly and continued his tirade. "It's about time we put your fucking family where it belongs, and he knows it."

I clenched my teeth to keep from whimpering and clutched the back of Ivan's shirt. The idiot Anton made a show of leaning around Ivan to leer at me. "She's pretty, your little whore," he said.

Ivan swung the bottle and cracked the kid in the side of the head with it and I couldn't say I was displeased. Anton staggered, clutching his ear as his friends surged forward. Before I could scream, we were surrounded, but not by Anton's crew. Four men I recognized convened around us, closing ranks in front of me and on either side of Ivan.

Anton's group dropped back almost to the water's edge, but stupid Anton cradled his face and continued to glare at Ivan, and now his small army.

"Choose wisely," Ivan said. "I've heard it's a far worse fate than death to lose a child."

My hand went to my stomach and I smothered a gasp. Ivan barely glanced at me before turning his dark stare back on Anton. "I won't dishonor the truce between our families," he continued. "Don't be stupid and end that truce."

Ivan and his men stepped forward as one and there was a brief flash of dawning comprehension on Anton's face that he was about to get his ass kicked all the way to West Palm if he didn't cut his losses. Clearly enraged and embarrassed, he tossed out a few more curses as he backed away to join his friends, who were practically running away up the beach.

All the adrenaline drained out of me as soon as Anton and his gang were out of sight. I kept my hand on my now churning stomach, unable to shake Ivan's words. I was already so attached to this baby, who was barely the size of a plum. How could I survive if something happened to it? Ivan sent his men back into the darkness where they'd materialized and I slumped into Ivan's arms once we were alone again.

He tried to ease me back onto the blanket, but I stood stiffly in his arms. He stroked my back and whispered soft words into my hair. I couldn't go back to our fun evening and pretend nothing happened like he wanted and I pressed my hand against my belly.

"That kid was the son of one of your enemies?" I asked. He nodded against the top of my head. "Will our child be someone's enemy one day?"

His hand stilled against my back as I waited for his honesty, for the first time not wanting it. "Probably. But our child won't be an idiot."

He pulled back to search my eyes, then looked off into the darkness where I now knew his men were guarding us. I also knew the night was over. We walked toward the hotel and as soon as we neared where his men were posted, he roughly took my arm and dragged me the rest of the way while they followed. Someone had brought his car from where we originally parked it and it waited for us in front of the hotel. He didn't bother opening the door for me this time, only barked for me to get in.

The drive back to my prison cell was silent and as soon as we pulled in front of the huge mansion, I jumped out of the car and hurried ahead of him. I slammed myself in my room, staring at the door, counting the seconds until he burst in. We'd have a fight and then start tearing each other's clothes off. Disgusted with myself, I still couldn't wait to get my hands under that crisp white shirt and all over his hard chest. I needed him to make me forget the fear I'd felt on the beach. I just needed him.

I finally got undressed and crawled into my big empty bed on my own, more disgusted with myself at how disappointed I was that he never came.

Chapter 12 - Ivan

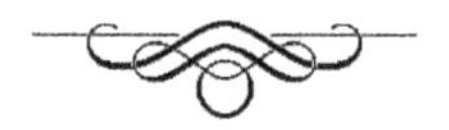

I paced the length of my room, down the hall from Reina's. I was furious with myself for foolishly allowing her to be put in danger, all to see a smile on her face. To spoil her like the queen she was. Now she was angry with me and frightened for our child on top of everything. I was used to her anger, but I couldn't stand seeing the realization about our child's future status cause all the color to drain from her face. Steal the light from her eyes. She still didn't have enough faith in me to never let her or my heir ever be in danger.

And why should she when I practically walked right into that situation tonight? I knew that Sergey Balakin's promises meant less than nothing, and the proof walked right up to my wife and looked at her as if she was dirt. Called her names and scared her. I struck the wall until my fist went through it. Ignoring the blood on my knuckles, I only wished I'd hit Anton Balakin with that champagne bottle until his head had caved in like the drywall in front of me. I should have cast my vote with Nikolai and Yuri, but I let Aleksei's siren call of peace sway me. I wanted the best outcome for the child in Reina's belly and I'd ended up putting both of them in danger.

I called up Aleksei to rage at him, making sure he understood exactly what was at stake. "Find out if your truce is still in order," I shouted as soon as he answered. "If not, all hell is going to break loose."

He tried to calm me down, but I ended the call and tossed my phone down to resume pacing. I missed Reina and wished I'd gone to her room. But I was too angry, and there was no denying the devastation in her eyes when faced with the reality that our child would one day be in my position. Would one day carry on the Morozov name, as king, just as I did now. I couldn't ease that burden for her, nor could I change our child's fate. I had too much pride in what my own father and I accomplished over the years.

I needed to give Reina space to come to terms with all that no matter how much I craved her body. Once things were more secure with the Balakins I could slowly start introducing her around as my wife, make things public so she didn't have to stay cooped up all the time. I knew she hated it, and I hated for her to be miserable. In my heart of hearts, I wanted her to embrace us being together and stop viewing herself as a prisoner.

My phone pulled me out of my thoughts, and I stopped pacing to see it was a video call from the Balakin head himself. I accepted the call, and Anton's bruised face filled the screen. The view pulled back, and a hand struck him hard enough to jerk his head back, obviously not the first strike he'd received that night.

"Tell him," a voice I recognized from our last meeting. His father, Sergey, he sounded angry.

Anton cleared his throat, looking like he wanted to spit. "I wasn't ordered to do what I did. I acted alone and my father knew nothing about it." His wild glare cut to the side and his jaw tensed. Another ruthless backhand landed across his cheek. "I—I'm sorry for what I did."

The hand shoved him away and the camera turned to reveal Sergey. He looked grim and haggard. It couldn't be fun to have to deal with such a shameful member of your organization, worse that it was his son. Just like I'd told Reina, I swore to myself that our child would never be such a fool.

"Our truce is still in effect," he rasped. "Anton won't be a problem to you anymore. I'll meet at any time to discuss it further if you need me to."

I admired him for trying to stay strong despite having to grovel due to his worthless offspring. "Aleksei will contact you again about that," I told him, keeping my voice cold and devoid of any emotion. Let him wonder if I was truly satisfied with his attempt to make amends.

He nodded, his chin trembling. "Are we good, Morozov?"

"For now."

I ended the call and sunk into the nearest chair, shocked at how relieved I was. No matter how angry I got, avoiding a war was always going to be the best way to proceed if I was to keep Reina and the baby safe. No matter the cost to our businesses, that was my only concern. I put my head in my hands. Were my feelings for Reina and our unborn baby making me soft?

Chapter 13 - Reina

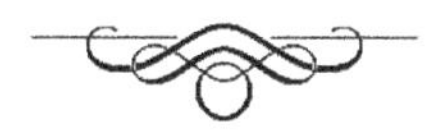

I woke up the next morning to find I was still in a bad mood about the night before. Sick to death of worrying about Ivan or my status in his life, I asked for my breakfast out on my balcony to hopefully watch the seagulls dive bomb the boats on the waterway. Even poor Hetty suffered from my mood when I snapped at her that I didn't care what I ate for breakfast.

"Surprise me," I said sarcastically, kicking the magazine pile so that they all slid off the table and fanned out on the floor.

Feeling like the world's worst brat, I stacked them back up and rearranged the rattan furniture while I waited for my food. I fluffed the cheery floral cushions and made sure all the bright, potted flowers were watered. Everything I was surrounded by was beautiful and comfortable. There was no reason to be so miserable, or at least so ungrateful. Ivan could have just as easily stuffed me in a dank basement somewhere until the baby was born.

By the time Hetty returned with my breakfast I felt more like a human and was able to thank her without sounding like I had razors in my throat. Then I uncovered the silver tray and the shaky house of cards that was my mood came tumbling down all over again. It was pigs in a blanket, three pancakes, neatly rolled up in a row with perfectly browned sausages sticking out of the ends. I set the tray on the table and sat there staring at one of my favorite childhood meals as tears filled my eyes.

Since my mother died when I was little, my dad had to be both parents. He never remarried or even dated, telling me when I was a teenager that no one could ever replace my mom, the love of his life. He was happy to take care of me, and he did his best, but he wasn't the best cook. It was something I teased him about, but he still endeavored to always give me home cooked dinners most nights. Most of the time they weren't that great. What was great were his pancakes every Sunday. Pigs in a blanket, just like the meal in front of me, albeit not on a silver platter or with cantaloupe cut up to look like roses.

"I'm so sorry, Dad," I whispered, feeling responsible for his case still being unsolved.

Maybe I shouldn't have come to Florida. I should have stayed and ridden the detectives to figure out who killed him. I was a coward, afraid of the unrelenting grief that refused to let up as long as I was still there.

I had to keep up my strength for the baby, so I forced down the pancakes. They were delicious, like everything prepared by Ivan's professional chef, but they didn't hold a candle to my dad's.

Ivan surprised me a little while later, breaking up the monotony of staring at the waterway. Even with my lingering anger over the night before and through the sadness of dredged up memories, I couldn't help being happy to see him.

"I'm going to give you some self-defense lessons," he said, leading me into the living area.

I watched him shove aside the couch, admiring his rippling muscles. Then it hit me that he might not be trying to help me pass the time.

"Am I in danger?"

He took my hands and kissed each one. "Not as long as I'm alive, my queen. But it's a good skill to have."

He opened up a gym bag and spread out a mat, first showing me how to break free from holds, then he taught me how to take down an attacker. He was as gentle with me as if I were a newborn kitten, and a good teacher. Soon I was able to get him off his feet with an ankle sweeping move.

"Now, I'll grab you from behind," he said, making my already accelerated heart rate speed up even more. And not just from the tough workout. He looked scary, and I liked it. Maybe because I knew he was no danger to me. At least I hoped not.

I shivered and he rubbed the goosebumps off my arms. "I'm going to hold you tight, my queen. I want you to think about how important you are to me and how devastated I'd be if I ever lost you. And fight accordingly."

Instead of doing what he instructed, which was to get my shoulder under his armpit and use momentum to bring him over and down, I just stood there, frozen by his words. He leaned down and tipped my chin up, asking why I wasn't doing what he told me.

"I'm important to you?" I asked, barely able to get the words out through my tightened throat.

He laughed. "How can you ask such a thing?"

I snorted right back, glaring up at him. "How can I not? You're hot and cold. If it weren't for the baby—"

He turned me in his arms and held me close. "Reina, do you know I couldn't get you off my mind those weeks we were apart? When you showed up in my club to give me the news, it was the happiest I'd felt in a long time."

I was stunned and could only stare at him in wonder. This wasn't a declaration of love, but he was spending time with me, showing me how to stay safe. Because he cared.

"Okay," I said simply, smiling.

Then I turned in his grasp and wedged my shoulder into his chest and flipped him. I was shocked when it worked, despite him being a foot taller than me, and laughed down at him lying flat on his back on the ground.

"You're a bloodthirsty one," he said, sitting up and beaming at me proudly.

I joined in with his laughter, unable to believe this was the ruthless crime lord I'd caught overseeing a torture session not that long ago. "Let me flip you again. That was so fun."

He finally got tired of landing on the mat, and he folded my hand into a fist. "It's time to learn to hit." He held his palms up and I took a jab, my arm recoiling when my fist hit his solid hand. I rubbed my knuckles and he shook his head. "Someone's face is going to be much harder and your aim is to knock them out so you can get away. Hit harder."

"I don't want to hurt you," I said, making him chuckle.

"You can't hurt me, so give it your all. You must be serious when you're fighting for survival."

"Way to be reassuring," I said, my stomach flipping.

"Tell me you haven't wanted to really punch me. Not in all this time?"

Since I knew how much he valued honesty, I kept quiet and he burst out laughing. "Let it all out, my queen."

My fists flew, crashing into his palms as fast and hard as I could, all traces of my bad mood gone. Maybe I was bloodthirsty like he'd teased, but I pictured Ivan's hands being my father's killer, imagining I was taking shots at that person's face. I was breathless when Hetty interrupted us to remind me of my doctor's appointment.

"She's ready whenever you are."

I looked at Ivan hopefully. "Would you like to stay? I'm getting an ultrasound."

His whole face softened and he put the same hands I'd been pummeling lightly on my tiny bump. "Absolutely."

Dr. Freeman wheeled her equipment in and not for the first time I wondered how odd this was to her. Maybe she serviced all the mafia wives or maybe rich people in general couldn't be bothered to mix with regular sick people so she was used to making house calls. I watched as she set up the machine with growing excitement. These doctor visits were a highlight of my existence, being reassured that the baby was all right. The one perfect thing about my new, bizarre life was how much I couldn't wait to be a mom. The only time I felt normal and at peace was when Lynn and I were talking about baby things or when I was reading parenting books. Everything else was up in the air, but I was certain I was going to adore being a mother.

I settled onto the rolling table Dr. Freeman always brought and pulled up my shirt so she could put the gel on my stomach. Ivan stood beside me, taking in the equipment with a suspicious air. Dr. Freeman pressed the wand to my stomach and moved it around while I kept my eyes glued to the screen. I held my breath when it remained blank and quiet, feeling dread creep up my spine. I reached for Ivan and he took my hand, no longer scowling at Dr. Freeman but at the ultrasound screen.

My breath came out in a rush as a moving blob appeared and tears sprang to my eyes when I heard the rapid, steady heartbeat through the speakers. Ivan's hand tightened around mine and I spared a look at him to see him staring at the image of our baby.

"Can you tell if it's a boy or a girl yet?" I asked.

"It's a bit too soon for that," Dr. Freeman said, moving the wand to try to get different angles. "But everything looks and sounds good." She smiled at both of us. "Maybe in a few more weeks we'll know the sex."

"Let's keep it a secret," Ivan said, surprising me. "The fact it's healthy is the most important thing."

I was relieved to hear him say that, secretly frightened he might be disappointed if it wasn't a boy. He still stared at the screen with an inscrutable expression, even after Dr. Freeman took away the wand. She printed out some pictures, took my blood pressure, and packed up to leave.

Once she was gone, Ivan sat on the couch and pulled me onto his lap. "Tell me what you want more than anything else, Reina," he said. "Even though nothing can compare to what you're giving me, I want to try."

As touching as this was, thoughts of my father flooded back. He'd never get to see his grandchild, even though he should have been healthy and happy and as excited as I was. All the fun of the self-defense lesson was erased, along with my relief from another clean bill of health for the baby. All I felt was that same impotent anger and bone-crushing grief all over again. I scrambled off of Ivan's lap and ran for the balcony, barely getting the door shut behind me before I dissolved into tears.

Ivan followed me a moment later, gripping my shoulders and trying to get me to look at him. I shrugged away from him, inconsolably sobbing into my hands.

"Ah, Reina," he said, sounding as tortured as I felt. "Please don't ask me to let you go. You're mine, my sweet queen, and what's more, it's too dangerous."

He thought I was crying because he couldn't give me what he thought I most wanted. "It's not that," I said, trying to get myself under control. "It's nothing to do with you."

"Tell me what it is, then," he commanded.

I gripped the balcony railing and felt his hand on my back, soft and comforting. But I couldn't be comforted. I whirled to face him.

"Fifteen months ago my father was murdered. He owned a hardware store, just a little shop that got by because of lifelong loyal customers and the fact he was so helpful and knowledgeable about any tool you'd ever need. He was out back, just before closing one night, and someone shot him. Not a robbery—they just killed him. He was all I had…"

I trailed off, too wracked by sobs thinking about how he hadn't been found for hours. No one would take me seriously when I called the police to report he was late coming home and not answering his phone. He always answered my calls. I tried to tell Ivan how I'd finally gone looking for him, only to find him long dead in a pool of blood.

"And they still haven't found his killer. I don't think they're really even trying anymore," I finished, exhausted.

Ivan pulled me into his arms and stroked my back. I collapsed against his strong chest, accepting his comfort and feeling lighter after getting it all out. I wrapped my arms around his waist and held on.

"My father was assassinated by mobsters, so I can understand the loss," he said slowly, as if opening up to me was as difficult as prying open a rusty chest kept in the attic for too long. "I know what it's like to have him stolen unfairly by another person and to feel the rage at the injustice of it."

"This is all I want, Ivan," I told him. "Just for you to be sweet and let me in. It's awful, worrying and not knowing what's going on in your life."

He made a rumbling noise in his chest. When I tipped my head back, he leaned down to kiss me tenderly. "Always, my queen. I don't want you to worry about me."

"How can I not, when I never know what you're doing, except that it's probably dangerous?"

He frowned, then nodded. "I'll tell you what I can, from now on."

"That means so much to me," I sighed, standing on tiptoe to kiss him again.

The kiss grew heated, and my grip on him tightened as his hands roamed lower down my back. This was what I needed. It had been too long.

He pulled away with an apologetic look. "I'm sorry to leave you now. Believe me, I want to stay. But I have a meeting scheduled with the Balakin family to discuss the breach of our truce last night."

I was stunned he actually told me instead of just storming off. I pulled his face down for another kiss. "Come and find me as soon as you're back," I told him urgently. I wasn't embarrassed to admit how much I needed him after baring my soul the way I did.

"The moment I return," he promised, giving me a look that melted my panties.

After he was gone, I paced the length of my living room, deciding that staying in ignorance might have been a better option. I'd never been so worried about him before when I didn't know what was going on. Or maybe it was because suddenly the thought of losing him had somehow become unbearable.

CHAPTER 14 - IVAN

I met up with Aleksei at a bar halfway between my club and the hotel the Balakins operated out of. I wanted it to be neutral ground and hoped the amount of innocent bystanders at the small pub would keep things civil. I didn't trust Sergey or his wildcard son as far as I could throw either of them, but I didn't trust many people. My youngest brother, Yuri, was fed up and told us to call him when we had tax questions, and I didn't want Nikolai there, afraid he'd end up being the one who couldn't remain civil.

The entire time Sergey assured me he had his son under control, I kept my fists clenched in my lap, picturing the way he'd taunted my wife. But I couldn't explain the seriousness of the offense without admitting Reina was my wife and putting an even bigger target on her back. So I nodded and accepted his apologies. We hashed out a new deal that was mostly acceptable to both of us and Aleksei, and I stayed behind after Sergey left.

After the server left the vodka bottle on the table, I poured each of us a stiff drink. We tapped our shot glasses and swallowed the alcohol down in swift gulps, both of us glad the meeting was over and had gone relatively well. The fact none of us were delighted was just the nature of compromise, and since we had agreed not to obliterate them off the face of the earth for daring to enter our city, then they had to agree to keep their fingers out of our pies.

Aleksei made a face at the cheap vodka. "We should go back to your place where you have the good stuff from home," he said.

I snickered. "You were eight when we came here, I was ten. This is our home, Aleks. What do you really think about this nonsense with the Balakins?"

He poured himself another shot of the swill and shrugged. "I think it's just that. Nonsense. But I've grown tired of killing. I just want to make money hand over fist and find a wife like you did. What's it like to have someone at home every night that you can count on to have your back?"

I raised my eyebrows at that. "You're saying you want to settle down?"

My younger brother had a different woman every night of the week. The ones who didn't know his reputation went for his good looks, and the ones who did want a taste of his money and power. I could see why he might want someone he could count on. After all, I didn't miss my old life one bit. If only I was certain I could count on Reina. Sometimes it seemed like she cared, like the worry she showed when I left for this meeting, but if I gave her back her freedom, would she stay? Or would she be gone faster than a startled rabbit?

"Maybe in a year or two or five," he said, smiling when the pretty red-haired server came back to see if we wanted anything else.

I left him to flirt, wanting to get out of the dark bar. I promised Reina I'd get back as soon as I could and now that the tensions revolving around the truce were lessened, I could let my mind wonder what I wanted to do with her when I got home. I told my driver to meet me at the end of the block, since there was a jewelry shop a little way down the road. I'd been affected by the story of her father and wanted to do whatever I could to take her mind off of it. She had looked so lovely in the emerald bracelet I chose for her for our failed date night that I decided to get her matching earrings.

Inside the shop, I loitered near the engagement rings. The one she wore now had been chosen in haste and angrily shoved onto her finger, and I had no idea if she even liked it or not. She knew she'd face my wrath if she ever took it off, though. While I waited for the owner to bring his selection of antique jewels from the safe, I tapped out a few messages to my contacts in the mid-west. I didn't have much hope, because random crime was sadly a reality, but if there was anything I could do to put her mind at ease about her father's case, then I would do it.

"These should suit your needs very well, Mr. Morozov." The jeweler returned with several gold and emerald pieces on a velvet pad, explaining their worth and provenance.

There was a pair of eighty-year-old emerald and pearl earrings with a matching necklace I could picture against my wife's fair skin and bought them, making the shop owner a very happy man. I only hoped Reina's smile would be as big and I could hardly wait until she was naked on her bed so I could drape them across her soft skin.

On my way out, I noticed a kid's clothing store across the street, and hurried across, thinking a pair of baby booties would be sure to bring a smile to her face. Any one of my brothers would have rightfully rolled their eyes at me at how eager I was to please her. My little queen was making me ridiculously soft. Yes, I had to be getting soft, because as soon as I was surrounded by the tiny clothes, I felt a warm tug in my chest. I couldn't wait to hold my heir in my arms.

My phone buzzed annoyingly in my pocket as soon as both hands were filled with little outfits. I transferred them under my arm to see who was bugging me then let them flutter to the floor when I saw it was my home security number.

"What is it?" I marched outside, all thoughts of buying baby clothes gone in an instant. They wouldn't call me for no reason. My heart seized when I heard screaming in the background, and I raced toward my car. But no, it wasn't Reina's voice; it was Hetty, her maid. She was hysterical, and I could hardly hear what my head of security was saying.

"Can't you shut her up?" I snarled. "I can't hear what you're saying."

"Get home, sir," he yelled over the shrieks in the background.

I yanked my driver out of his seat, telling him he could hop in the back or find his own way back to the house. There was no way he'd get me there fast enough. I laid on the horn and barreled through every red light, my foot jamming the gas pedal to the floor. It still seemed like I was traveling in slow motion. What had made Reina's maid so upset? Finally, I screeched into my driveway, flying out of the car before it was fully stopped, and leaving the poor driver to lurch forward from the back to try to keep it from crashing into the fountain. Upstairs, my head of security and several of his men were searching the rooms. I found Hetty in a heap on Reina's living room floor, tearing at her clothes as she sobbed uncontrollably.

Blood. Blood on the floor, a trail of it leading to the balcony.

"Reina!" I bellowed. She'd come to me. She wouldn't dare defy such a shout.

Hetty pointed a shaking hand toward the balcony, one of Reina's favorite places to sit and watch the water. I hurried out there to see more splashes of red all over the marble rail and everything went quiet and still. I could barely see or hear or move. I'd seen the aftermath of violence plenty of times. I'd been the cause of it plenty more. But this time was different.

The security head caught up to me and everything jerked back to normal. "Where is Reina?" I reached to shake the man, who looked like he might be sick. Useless. "Where is Maksim, if you can't answer me?"

He brushed past me and pointed over the edge of the balcony. "Maksim is dead, sir."

I didn't believe it. I'd chosen him to guard Reina because he was as tough and strong as me, and I trusted him almost as much as one of my brothers. I looked over the side to see him hanging half off the concrete bird of paradise planter, his throat gaping open like a bright red jack-o-lantern's grin.

"Reina," I gasped. I didn't want to know.

"We can't find her, sir."

I glared at him to tell me the truth, to admit he was lying, then looked over the balcony again, expecting Maksim to jump up and tell me this was a very poor joke. But Maksim never moved. He was dead and now Reyna was gone.

Chapter 15 - Reina

I was reading a book on the balcony, probably the tenth one that week, whiling away the time until I could talk to Lynn on the phone or Ivan came back, whichever came first. I wasn't as unhappy as I was that morning and while I wished I at least had the freedom to roam around the property, I was pleased that Ivan was finally telling me where he was going and not just treating me like a sex object. That was progress, right?

I put the book down and closed my eyes, dreamily conjuring up ideas for when he got back. To be fair, I didn't one hundred percent mind the sex object part of our strange relationship. My daydream started to get pretty spicy when I was shaken out of it by a loud thump right below the balcony. No sooner had my eyes opened than a big, metal hook came flying over the edge, and seconds later, two men dressed in khaki fatigues with masks covering most of their faces climbed over the side.

I let out a shrill screech as one of them slammed me against the wall. "This will go better for you if you don't fight," he said menacingly.

All I could see were his eyes, grayish blue and full of malice, but I would have recognized that punk from the beach's arrogant, bratty voice anywhere. Anton. His partner burst through the door into the living area and I heard Hetty shout for help and then a crash. The thought of poor Hetty getting hurt because she had the misfortune to work for me pissed me off enough to forget how scared I was. I pulled my knee up sharply, getting him in the groin. Then I used my fist in the way I'd practiced with

Ivan, clocking him in the cheek with enough force to make his head snap back while he moaned in agony over his crotch injury.

Speaking of agony, Ivan hadn't been kidding when he said it hurt a lot worse hitting someone in the face than it did to hit his open palms. I feared my hand might be broken. I kicked him again, this time in the shin, and shoved past him into the house. I made it two steps in to see Maksim storming into my room with his gun raised, only to see him be struck over the head with a heavy copper urn by the other guy who'd been hiding by the door.

"You coward," I yelled, bending down to run at him like a bull.

I was just improvising at that point, scared half to death and mad as hell. I only got another two steps before Anton grabbed a handful of my hair and jerked me backwards. I fell to the floor and saw his foot coming toward me. Terrified he was going to boot me in the stomach, I curled up in a ball to protect the baby. Thinking I was down for the count, he went to help with Maksim, who was shaking his head and lurching to try to take down the one who'd nailed him with the urn. Hetty hurried to my side to pull me into the bedroom with her.

"We'll lock them out and call Mr. Morozov," she said, helping me up. "Security is coming, we just need to hide."

As she dragged me toward the bedroom, I saw that Maksim had his hand on his gun again and thought this might be over soon, and I wouldn't need to hide. I was so mad I didn't care if those two bastards' brains ended up all over my cream leather sofa. In fact, I kind of hoped that would happen.

"Maksim, look out!" I shouted, horrified to see the one behind him pull out a knife that was so long it almost looked like a pirate sword.

With a smooth, sure movement, he slashed the blade cleanly across my guard's throat, and as Maksim gurgled and reached for his neck to try to stay the gush of blood, the horrible, masked man shoved him across the room toward the balcony. I was frozen in terror as he pushed Maksim right over the side. A second later, the loud crash that could only be his body hitting the terrace below shook me out of my stupor.

Hetty and I locked eyes and raced for the bedroom. Where in the hell was the mansion security? Hetty slammed into the closed door and wrenched it open, trying to push me in ahead of her. But then a big arm wrapped around my neck and a damp, sickly sweet smelling cloth got smashed over my nose and mouth. I reached for Hetty but was getting pulled backwards, away from her. That big knife swung at her, missing her face by only an inch. She screamed and swerved away and that was the last thing I remembered before everything went hazy, then completely black.

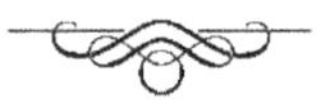

I woke up somewhere dark and damp, feeling stiff and sore, and with a raging headache. I tried to stretch out my aching back to find I couldn't move my arms at all. They were wedged behind me, tied to a pole that dug into my spine. No amount of tugging or jerking could get them free. Panic bubbled close to the surface, but I shoved it down. The longer my eyes were open, the more I could see. The place wasn't pitch dark, there were small, rectangular windows high up on the walls that let the light come through. It didn't seem like daylight, more like street lamps. I sat on a bare concrete floor and my hands had a little leeway, enough to get slightly more comfortable. My legs jutted out in front of me and thankfully they were free, so if I had the chance, I could kick someone if they got close enough.

I was probably in a basement, based on the high windows and the fact the place was completely empty. If I craned my neck, I could see what might have been the railing to some stairs. It helped to calmly take stock, rather than freak out. I'd just go over all the facts of my situation.

I already knew who nabbed me. That dumb kid of Ivan's rival. It had to be revenge against Ivan for humiliating him, or maybe his father wanted to make a power play. Either way, it probably wasn't going to end well for me. I curled my legs up around my stomach, trying not to cry. So much for remaining calm. This was a real prison, not my beautiful suite at the mansion. I squeezed my eyes shut, wishing I was back there, then gasping as I remembered that Maksim was most likely dead, and maybe Hetty had been killed as well.

I took several deep, slow breaths, to calm myself, not wanting to throw up since then I'd have to sit in it. I tried screaming, but my voice only echoed in the large, empty room and nobody answered. I lapsed into silence and tried not to think at all. After a while, footsteps on the stairs startled me out of my fear induced trance. I pulled at my binding again, wincing at the sores that were forming on my wrists, then sat very still when the footsteps stopped at the bottom of the stairs.

"You can still save your sorry lives if you let me go," I yelled, pleased that I sounded braver than I felt. "That's you, isn't it, Anton?"

The silence was unnerving, but it was even worse when he strode out of the shadows, pulling off his mask. "So, no need for this anymore," he said, tossing it aside.

He stopped in front of me and hauled back his foot to slam it into my thigh. It hurt but thanks to my extra padding, I didn't think it did any real damage and I was able to stare defiantly up at him. His face was a mess of cuts and bruises, which made me smile. It wasn't justice for Maksim, but I liked thinking this jerk had paid for something he did.

"He's going to make you suffer before he kills you," I said. "You don't look like you need any more bruises."

He ran a hand over his face. "This? This was all for show. I barely felt a thing."

"You'll feel it from Ivan," I said.

He dropped down to leer at me, roughly grabbing my chin when I recoiled from him. "I don't know why you're so important to the Morozov king, but you must be." He shoved my shoulder to the side and wrenched my rings off my finger, holding them so close to my face my eyes crossed. "Are these trinkets to keep you spreading your legs without complaining too much?"

I kicked at him and threw my head forward, hitting him in the bridge of his nose. He yelped and plastered his hand to my forehead, knocking me into the brick wall behind me. For a second I saw stars.

"*I'm* going to make you suffer before he kills you," I said, changing my threat as I wished I could rub away the pain that bloomed at the back of my head.

He stood and paced back and forth. "Surely you're not his wife. You can't be. No wedding, no fanfare. So why the fuss?" He was babbling to himself as he tossed my rings from hand to hand and then stuffed them into his pocket. I kicked at him again, but he was out of range, and my fury over my rings went unheeded. He stopped and shook his head at me, swooping down so fast it took my breath, and the last bit of my courage. His eyes were dark with hatred and it was all focused inches from my face. He wrapped his hand around my throat and squeezed. Who are you?" His grip tightened until black spots appeared in my peripheral vision. Just as quickly as he grabbed me, he let go and stood, sneering down at me once more. "I suppose we'll know soon enough if he takes the bait and comes for you."

I choked and thrashed against the ties at my wrists as he marched away, muttering something to the silent man who'd waited at the foot of the stairs while he taunted me. His ominous threat made me forget all about my rings, and even the pain in my head as I struggled to get my breath back. I curled into a ball as best I could, staring at the dim light coming through the windows, not sure what to hope for.

If Ivan came for me, he'd fall into their trap and might get hurt or worse. I couldn't think about worse. If he didn't come, what would become of me and the baby?

"Oh, Ivan," I whimpered, sinking into despair as the lights outside eventually winked out, leaving me in total darkness.

Chapter 16 - Ivan

Every last member of my security staff turned the house and grounds upside down and inside out while I conducted my own frantic search with Dmitri. My brothers were either on their way or looking into what might have happened. They were the only ones I trusted even a little bit at the moment, because I was finding it difficult to believe my home had been so easily infiltrated, my wife stolen from under my very nose.

Every time I passed a member of the house staff while I looked under beds and in closets, I had to wonder if that was the person who betrayed me. And to whom and for how much? How much was my queen worth?

"She's not here, Ivan," Dmitri said, coming from the back to meet me in the kitchen.

The chef and head housekeeper perched on barstools at the wide, granite island, looking worried and confused. They were my only permanent staff besides security, and I'd ordered them to stay put, making them believe they might be in danger by someone who could still be on the property. For all I knew when I shouted the order, it was true. I prayed it was true because that would mean Reina was still here with her captor, and I could tear his head off before I gathered her safely into my arms.

"Did you search the shed?" I snapped at Dmitri. "What about the greenhouse?" I started to push past him, but he put his hand on my shoulder.

"She's not here," he repeated.

I slammed my fist onto the unyielding granite island, making the frightened chef and housekeeper jump. I rounded on them, demanding once again to know if they saw or heard anything out of the ordinary after I left. Anything at all.

They shook their heads. The housekeeper, a woman who'd worked for me for ten years, started to cry.

"What about your girls?" I asked. She had helpers who regularly came to do the menial cleaning tasks.

"They're not in until Thursday. Mr. Morozov, I'm so sorry about your guest."

I hit the counter again and strode out of the kitchen with Dmitri on my heels. The fact they thought Reina was merely a houseguest tore at my heart to the point I almost couldn't stand. I didn't have time for self-recrimination now, though. There would be time to set everyone straight when Reina was found. And she would be found.

But would she be safe? Alive? If no one knew she was my wife, they couldn't know she was pregnant. I nearly doubled over with fear for my child. Our child. I wanted them both back. Thankfully rage overtook the fear and grief that threatened to topple me.

"Someone on the inside has to be part of this," I said.

Dmitri nodded. "Agreed. Who do you suspect?"

"Everyone," I growled.

I found the head of security and ordered him to stop the search and have his men report to me. A few minutes later the four of them stood in a line in front of me. "How did this happen?" I bellowed. "How did someone stroll onto the grounds, kill my cousin, and take—"

I stopped abruptly, waiting for their answer. Waiting to see what they'd confess to knowing, and if any of them slipped up and knew more than they should. Not even Dmitri or Maxim knew about my marriage. Only my brothers knew and I hadn't gone so far over the edge as to suspect any of them. Yet.

One of the security guards had been patrolling the back wall and hadn't seen a thing. Did that mean they'd waltzed right in through the front? The man who was supposed to be guarding the front had been working on the security feeds, which had been cutting in and out over the last few days. The next one was physically checking the cameras that were everywhere and had been on the roof above the front door.

"So there's nothing on the security feeds?"

They shook their heads dismally, stealing my last bit of hope for a lead. I rounded on the head.

"And where were you during this?"

"I—uh—I was out by the road, sir. I walked down the drive."

It was a solid five minute walk to the main road. "Checking the cameras out there?"

His eyes flickered, as if he was going to jump on this suggestion. When he nodded, I knew he was lying. I reached for his throat and squeezed. None of his men jumped to his aid. They knew better.

"What were you doing so far from the house?"

He closed his eyes and sighed, and I smelled it then. "Smoking," he admitted.

I shoved him away in disgust. Was it pure incompetence or actual malice? Had he been paid to be away from the house? As much as I wanted to bash some heads in my frustration, I couldn't start killing people for no reason, not when I might need to wring more information out of them.

"Get to your office and stay there until I need you," I shouted.

Three of them scurried away like scared mice, but the head lingered. "Should we alert the police?" he asked.

I punched him in the face and strode out of the room with Dmitri on my heels. "Keep an eye on everyone," I told him, wanting to be alone for a moment. "I need to make some calls."

When he was gone, I shut myself into my office and got Sergey Balakin on a video call. The moment his face filled my screen, I roared. "Where is she?"

His eyes widened. "Who, Ivan? What are you talking about?"

He looked sincerely confused and shocked by my rage. "Someone invaded my home and kidnapped a guest. A guest who had better not be harmed."

He shook his head, his brows shooting together. He turned his face away from his phone and shouted to someone to find his son. "I'll look into this," he said. "Don't do anything rash."

"You'd better find him before I do," I warned, ending the call.

He was either a good actor or truly didn't have any part in this. But that didn't mean his foolish son didn't. I called Aleksei for an update and he had men with their ears to the ground all over the city. I started to call Nikolai, but my hand shook so badly, I slammed the phone onto my desk. The thought of how frightened Reina must be made me sink into a chair and put my head in my hands. I prayed she was all right, the first time I'd beseeched God since I was a small boy. If anything happened to her, I vowed to burn this city to the ground to find out who did it.

There was a sharp knock at the door and I stood, calling for the person to enter. Nikolai pushed through, dragging a man by the arm. I cast around in my memory to retrieve a name to put to the terrified face.

"Reynaldo?" I asked.

Nikolai shoved the man forward so that he stood in front of me, eyes cast down. "That's right," my brother said. "He's not Russian, but I thought he was trustworthy. He's been on my team for about five years now."

"You have news for me?"

"I know who your mole is," the man sniveled, not meeting my eyes. "I just found out, I swear it. I was going to tell Nikolai as soon as he returned from your meeting."

I looked at Nikolai, who shrugged. "I'm not so sure about that because Reynaldo here just bought a fancy new car last week. Quite a bit out of his price range, which was why I started keeping an eye on him."

I slammed my hand into his chest, sending him rocking backward. Nikolai steadied him and I pounded my fist into his face three times in quick succession.

"What do you know?" I demanded.

He shook his head, sending blood drops flying. I thought of Maksim's blood upstairs and drew back my fist again. He flinched. "I can tell you who your mole is, but I swear I'm not a part of this. I don't know where—"

He stopped himself and I cut my glance away to see Nikolai subtly shake his head. "All he should know is that your house was breached," he told me.

Which meant he would have had no idea that anyone was taken, let alone my queen. "Round up his family," I ordered.

Reynaldo crumpled to his knees, tears mingling with the blood that flowed down his face. "No, please," he cried. "Please leave my family out of it and I'll tell you everything. I know my own life is over."

I stared at the man and sighed, waiting for his hysteria to pass. "I'll be the judge of that when I get what's mine back."

Nikolai hauled the man up and shoved him into a chair while I crossed my arms and impatiently waited for information I hoped would be useful to find my wife.

Chapter 17 - Reina

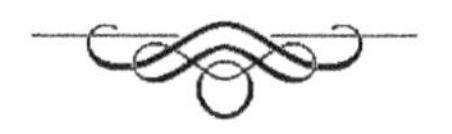

I woke up in the same sorry position, not sure how much time had passed, but light streamed through the small, grimy windows again. At least I was no longer in utter darkness, but it wasn't much to be grateful for. Once again I tried to free myself, but the ropes only dug into my wrists even more. I tried sliding upward on the pole I was tied to, but ended up twisting my ankle painfully and sat back down with a hard thump on the dusty floor. It was hard not to sink into hopelessness, and on top of everything else, my stomach rumbled with hunger, then turned over in a bout of nausea. I would have killed for a dry cracker.

No matter what I thought about to distract myself from sinking into despair, it just made it worse. Thinking about the crackers made me think of all the gourmet meals I'd been given at Ivan's house. Then I'd think about Ivan, alternating between missing him, wanting to scream at him, and worrying about him if he found me. Worrying about myself if he didn't find me.

My brain snapped to a halt, gripped with fear, when I heard footsteps on the stairs. For one, glorious second I thought it might be Ivan and his men coming to bust me out of this nightmare, but it was only Anton and a few of his cronies. One look at Anton's sneer, and I had the overwhelming certainty that I was about to die.

Deep anger blotted out my fear or any sadness I had about this fact. A lot of that anger was directed at Anton for being the kind of person who'd kill a pregnant woman in a basement for nothing more than being schooled for being an obnoxious brat. A good deal of the anger went to

Ivan, for forcing me to marry him and treating me like I was his property. Property to be stolen and passed around by his enemies.

Most of all, I was pissed at myself. I should have tried harder to get away from him when I was safely in the mansion with Maksim barely paying attention to me. Why didn't I slip away when I had the chance? I whined and complained about being in a prison, but this was a real prison, not the mansion. Deep down, I liked the luxury, and I loved Ivan's attention. Now it was too late, and I was going to die like Maksim did, or in a more drawn out way, since I'd taunted the young upstart.

At least I'd get to see my father again when it was all over. I squeezed my eyes shut to keep the tears that were welling from leaking out when I remorsefully thought about the baby. If only I hadn't been so stupid, it could have had a chance at life.

I opened my eyes when the footsteps stopped in front of me, and looked up at Anton. Two men stood a few feet behind him, one of them menacingly wielding a baseball bat. My mind jolted back to the scene in Ivan's shed and the damage that bat had done to the person they were interrogating. But what information could they hope to wring out of me? I barely knew anything about my husband's business. I didn't even know his middle name.

It took all my concentration to keep from crying or begging for my life, or admitting I was pregnant and pleading for the baby. I knew what kind of people these were. I was married to the same type of people. At least I'd go out with my pride intact and I refused to give them any more ammunition to use against Ivan. I snickered at the fact I still cared what happened to him at the same time I wanted to slap him if I ever saw him again.

Oh, Ivan.

Anton leaned over, getting much too close to my face again. "What's funny?" he asked.

I merely glared at him until he finally shrugged and moved away. Point to me. He flicked open a pocket knife and leaned back down and my breath caught in my throat. This was it, then. Ultimately, Anton had won. He leaned closer and dragged the tip of the blade down my cheek. The point dug in under my jaw and I closed my eyes, waiting for the burst of pain that would end my life. He laughed, and instead of stabbing me in the jugular, which might have at least been quick, he continued running the knife down my neck, slicing at my top. I started to shake, fearing the pain when he finally found a spot to make the first cut. But he only slashed the ropes around my wrists and jerked me to standing. I was still alive. For now. My legs had trouble adjusting to being upright after so long and I struggled to keep up as he dragged me across the basement and up the stairs behind his henchmen.

He pushed me through the doors into a brightly lit room that was even scarier than the dark, empty basement. It seemed to be an office of some sort, but everything was covered in sheets of plastic, decked out to make it easier to keep evidence of a murder to a minimum. Even the lone window had plastic taped over it. He really didn't want to have to wipe up any blood. He shoved me into a chair, the heavy plastic sheeting making a crinkling sound when I hit the seat. Glancing at his men, he paced back and forth in front of me.

"You seem antsy," I taunted, throwing caution to the wind. I was in a murder room, for goodness' sake. My only hope was to buy time at this point. And have the satisfaction of making him as angry as I was. "You should be nervous, Anton. Ivan knows everything, and it's only a matter of time before you get your comeuppance for taking me."

The words were hollow, but my voice came across as brave, anyway. Sweat broke out on his brow as he continued to pace the small room. If only it was just me and him and not two other, weapon-wielding muscle men. I really thought I was mad enough to have a fair shot in a fight with Anton.

There was a light knock at the door, one of the silly rhythmic knocks that kids did for their secret clubs. Anton looked at the door, shocked, clearly not expecting anyone. The two other men stiffened, the one aiming his gun and the other holding up his baseball bat.

"Who the fuck is that?" Anton asked, staring at the door.

The next moment, there was an explosive sound of shattering glass and a man burst in through the window off to the side of me, tearing through the plastic sheeting. I was too stunned and so happy to see my husband to utter his name. He'd really found me. It hadn't been idle boasting. Somehow Ivan had found me. It struck me that I'd been able to be so brazen because I never really doubted it. He landed on the floor as gracefully as a cat and raised his gun.

Before Anton's men could turn around, he took them out with two well-aimed shots in rapid succession. Another man kicked through the door, aiming his gun on Anton as his men dropped to the floor with blood oozing from the holes in their heads. Good thing there was all that plastic. Ivan turned to point his own gun at his young nemesis.

"It's over," he said, voice as cold as ice and the sweetest sound I ever heard.

"Like hell," Anton muttered.

Panicked at having two guns trained on him, he leaped and grabbed me by my shirt, yanking me in front of him. His arm snaked around my neck and squeezed just like a python. He snapped open his pocket knife with his free hand and jabbed it against my cheek.

"I'll kill her," he said, backing toward the door. He stepped over one of his men's bodies, dragging me along with him. "Put your guns down or I swear I'll carve her up."

As I was being dragged backwards, I locked eyes with Ivan. I could read everything in that stormy blue gaze. A wellspring of promises lay there, behind the cold fury aimed at Anton. I nodded slightly, knowing I could trust him to the ends of the earth. He almost imperceptibly returned the nod, and I closed my eyes.

There was a deafening crack and Anton's grip slackened. He began to fall, his dead weight drawing me down with him. Before he collapsed completely on top of me, strong hands ripped me free and gathered me close to a body I knew all too well. I buried my face in Ivan's chest as he clutched at my hair, uttering soft words of reassurance.

He sent the other man to make sure the rest of the building was secure and to let the others who were still outside know what was going on. I wrapped my arms around him and held on as he guided me from the plastic room that had seen death after all, just not mine, thanks to Ivan.

As soon as we were outside in the sunshine, I pulled his head down to kiss him fiercely, then shoved him away and slapped him hard across the face. Tears started rolling down my cheeks, and I angrily swiped them away before pulling him close again. He held on, stroking my back and ducking down to kiss me.

"I'm sorry, Reina. I'm sorry, my queen," he repeated over and over.

I leaned back, gripping his shirt to tell him to stop. He'd saved me, that was all that mattered. I noticed my bare finger and gasped, running back into the warehouse again. The place was swarming with Ivan's men so I knew I was completely safe, but Ivan chased after me anyway. Back in the office, I looked at the three bodies with disgust, then leaned over Anton to search his pockets.

"Reina, what are you doing?" Ivan asked, probably concerned for my sanity after all that.

But I found what I wanted, pulling out my rings and holding them up triumphantly. "He thought he could take my rings from me," I said, kicking Anton's lifeless body before Ivan led me back outside once more.

I took his hand and pressed my diamond engagement ring and the simple gold band into his palm. He looked at me in confusion, his brow furrowed as if he might start bellowing until I held out my hand with my fingers spread. I waggled my ring finger and looked at him expectantly.

With a relieved smile, he put them back on. "Where they belong," he said.

I nodded fiercely and grabbed onto him again, never wanting to let go. "Take me home, Ivan. I want to go home."

Chapter 18 - Ivan

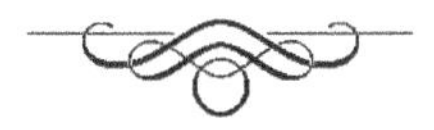

Once we got back to the house, I wouldn't let Reina out of my sight. Now that she was back with me, I wasn't going to lose her again. I was shocked that she seemed fine when I settled her in an armchair at the back of my office with a blanket and a bowl of berries instead of letting her go to my room. More than fine, actually, even while I "interviewed" everyone that Nikolai's employee, Reynaldo had named as possibly being untrustworthy. It was only the fact that his information had led us to saving Reina that saved his life, but he was going to be on a very tight leash for the foreseeable future.

So far, two of my security team had fled, disappearing as soon as Dmitri and I took off to the warehouse where Anton was keeping her. Aleksei had people combing the city for them, all of the airports under surveillance if they tried to leave the state. There wasn't a place on earth far enough away that I wouldn't track them down after what they allowed to happen in my home. To my woman.

They'll discover, the same as anyone who betrays me, that the money they received just wasn't worth what happened to them when I caught them, as I always did.

At first I was afraid I might have to postpone the interrogations to give Reina time to recover, and her steely calm made me think she was in shock from her ordeal. But my queen was made of sterner stuff than that, and she assured me she was fine. She shouldn't have cut such an intimidating figure, curled up in my oversized armchair and wrapped in a blanket at the back of the room, but every time I turned to check on her, she was glaring at the subject, probably scaring them worse than I was. I was bursting with pride for my little queen and done with caring who saw me dote on her. I'd never lay a rough hand on her again. The time she was gone and I feared I might be too late to save her and the baby was the worst hell I'd ever lived through. It wouldn't happen again, no matter who knew she was my wife.

I kept up my interrogations until I saw her head nodding toward her chest and the next time I peeked at her, her book had fallen from her hands. I called Dmitri and Nikolai in to continue on without me while I took her upstairs, but when I tried to lift her, she shook herself awake, giving the person currently being questioned a glare so cold, it could have rivaled one of mine.

"I'm perfectly fine," she said, picking up her book again. "Keep working."

I smiled at her to show her how proud I was of her, but scooped her into my arms all the same. "Dmitri and Nikolai can handle it for now," I told her. She frowned and looked like she might argue, wanting to get all the traitors as badly as I did. But not at the expense of her health. "You need to rest for the baby," I said in a low voice.

She nodded, knowing I was right, and relaxed against my chest. Just where I liked her to be. We passed her suite, shut up tight until it could be thoroughly cleaned. She shuddered and looked away.

"You never have to go back in there if you don't want to," I promised. "You'll stay in my bed from now on."

She sighed, then her eyes flew wide. "Hetty?" she asked. "They put something over my face, and I passed out. Is she all right?"

"Your maid is safe and sound. I sent her on a holiday with her family in Jamaica for a while, but she'll be back."

"She's my friend," Reina said. "She tried to save me when she could have run and hid on her own."

"She'll be well rewarded, my queen, don't you worry about that."

I nudged open my door and she gave one last long look down the hallway and stiffened in my arms. "Maksim," she whispered. "I was so mean to him."

I hurried into my room and set her feet on the floor, gathering her close as she collapsed against me, bitter tears streaming down her cheeks. I took a deep breath, knowing the pain of losing my cousin would hit me eventually. We all knew the life we led would most likely end in violence, likely even pain. It was still hard. Right now, I had to focus on Reina, not my own feelings.

"He was proud to be able to serve you," I said, rubbing her back. "He wouldn't want you to cry."

She drew in a big, shaky breath and let it out, blinking away the last of her tears. "All right, if you say so."

"I do. And while you're doing what I say, how about you get a nice, hot shower."

A tremor of a smile crossed her face as she nodded. "That sounds wonderful. I-I was tied up on the floor…"

I had to turn away so she wouldn't see the rage flash in my eyes. Anton may have gotten what he deserved, but there were still people out there that needed to pay for her suffering.

In the bathroom, I helped her get out of her clothes, angry at myself for not thinking to let her change sooner. Running my hands down her smooth skin, I inspected for any injuries, then ran the shower until steam billowed out from behind the glass door.

"I'll be right here," I told her, when she gave me a lingering look.

It only took a moment before I couldn't stand it any longer and stripped off my own clothes. Pulling the door back, I stepped under the hot, stinging spray with her, reaching for the soap to suds her back. I massaged her shoulders as her head dropped forward, and I could hear her contented sigh over the rush of the shower. Directing her to close her eyes, I lathered her hair, carefully rinsing the grime of her imprisonment down the drain.

"I won't let anything bad happen to you again," I swore, standing behind her and letting my hands settle on her stomach. "Or the baby."

She leaned back against me and reached up to run her fingers through my damp hair. Twisting her face up to me, I leaned down to give her a kiss. She arched her perfect ass against my quickly rising cock and moaned softly against my lips.

As much as I wanted her, she'd been through a lot and was exhausted. I had to control my own desires and restrain myself. Pulling away, I turned her to face me. Blinking moisture out of her big doe eyes, she searched my face. She was so, so beautiful. She stood on her toes beneath the spray and wrapped her arms around my neck.

"Ah, my sweet queen. I love you so much." My heart soared at finally saying the words I'd been fighting for so long. "I adore you, Reina." She smiled and pulled my head down for another kiss and my cock jumped against her belly. Once again I moved back. "Ignore that."

She smiled wickedly and ground against me harder. "What if I don't want to?" Her hand slid down my chest to grip my shaft. "Don't you want to ask me what I want right now?"

My breath was trapped in my throat as I stared at my soaking wet, gorgeous wife. "Tell me what you want," I demanded.

"You know, Ivan. You know exactly what I want."

I did, and it was what I most desired as well. I picked her up, dragging her body against mine as I hauled her against the tiled wall. She wrapped her legs around my waist and clung to my shoulders. I was deep inside her before her gasp was fully past her lips. All the fear and anger while I frantically searched for her disintegrated as her mouth met mine, her moans mingling with my panting breaths. This felt good. This was heaven.

But I wanted more for my queen. We had a lifetime together to roughly fuck in the shower. Right now I wanted to lavish her the way she truly deserved. With my cock still buried deep in her tight pussy, I groaned and carried her out of the shower. I managed to grab a towel and drape it around her shoulders.

"Ivan," she said, trying not to laugh at my fumbling antics. "What are you doing?"

"Wait and see, darling queen of mine."

Her giggles as I carried her to the bed were a tonic to my soul. I never wanted to see her cry again, at least not today. I laid her on her back and settled between her thighs, staring into her eyes as I pushed her strands of hair off her face.

"You didn't think this through, did you?" she asked.

While I loved the music of her laughter, I wasn't trying to put on a comedy show. And no, I hadn't thought it through. She made me wild, she made me thoughtless. She made me feel like I'd never really felt before.

"What do you do to me, Reina?" I asked, pulsing inside her.

"Tell me," she urged, cupping my face.

I rested my head on her shoulder, feeling exposed and raw. "You make me happy."

She grabbed me in a tight hug, squeezing her thighs around my hips. "Oh, Ivan." She wasn't laughing as she ran her finger down the side of my jaw. "You make me happy, too." Her brows drew together in a mock scowl. "Or you would, if you'd get back to what you started."

I slid down her body, kissing her as I went. She arched her back as I spent some time coaxing her nipples to taut peaks, and sighed blissfully as I reached the crux of her thighs.

"This is what you get when you complain," I said, gliding my tongue along the length of her slick pussy.

Her hands gripped the covers as her hips rose to meet my questing tongue. "Then prepare to hear me complain a whole lot more," she said breathlessly.

I could have happily lived the entire rest of my life hearing nothing but her complaints, but I meant to hear nothing but praise by the time I was done with my little queen.

Chapter 19 - Reina

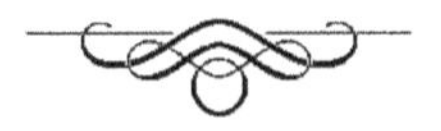

Lying in bed with Ivan, I was on the cusp of falling asleep, but desperate to stay awake to revel in the afterglow of what he made me feel. Despite being physically exhausted, I was also strangely revitalized, as if my heart had been renewed. I should have been traumatized by everything I'd been through, but instead, I felt better than I had in ages. Since well before my father was killed, but truly, I didn't think I had ever been so happy in my entire life as I was in Ivan's arms. I didn't want to think about the horror of being trapped in that basement, or relive the deafening gunshots. I wanted to stay right there with Ivan, and why shouldn't I?

He loved me. That was what I wanted to keep reliving. The moment he said he loved me. I turned to get closer to him and smiled against his chest as he curled his arm tighter around me.

This gorgeous, powerful man loved me? He didn't just want to keep me around because I was carrying his heir? Every fiber of my being wanted to believe it, but how could I? I was no one special.

I looked up at him at the same time he looked at me, surprised I was still awake. But how could I sleep when I wanted to bask in his love and wish with all my heart that it was real.

"Tell me what you want, Reina," he said.

I wanted to tell him I loved him, too, but something stopped me. What if he was just relieved the baby was all right? Sure, he cared about me, was definitely attracted to me, but love? The kind of love I'd always dreamed of as a little girl? I had never dreamed about being kidnapped and forced to marry, then kidnapped again and rescued and swept off my feet. It was a lot, and in the end, I was safe, but I still wasn't free. I belonged to Ivan, I had no choice in that, so did it really matter how either one of us felt?

"Reina." Ivan nudged me and I blinked.

"I want to learn how to shoot a gun," I said with no more hesitation. I waited for this to be the first thing he refused me. There was no way he was going to let me within a hundred yards of something that could help me gain my freedom.

He kissed my forehead. "Go to sleep, little queen."

I smiled and nestled back into the crook of his shoulder. So he'd gotten out of giving me what I wanted by completely ignoring the request. That was fine for the moment. With his hand trailing gently up and down my arm, I drifted into a dreamless sleep.

When I woke up, I was alone, but that was normal. Business as usual, even though I was in Ivan's room. I wondered briefly if he would move me back to my suite, or a different one, then wondered how long I had been asleep. With the blinds drawn, I had no idea if it was day or night. A woman who looked a little older than me stuck her head in the room and I sat up.

She offered me a bright smile and opened the blinds to reveal an even brighter day outside. "I'm Liz, I'll be filling in for your maid while she's on vacation."

She was so cheerful I wondered if she was just from a temp agency or if she was connected to Ivan's business in some way and used to everything that went on in crime families.

"What time is it?" I asked. "Uh, what day is it for that matter." I had lost track of time while I was in the basement.

"It's ten in the morning on Saturday," she said. "And it's eighty-seven degrees with no chance of rain."

I stifled a laugh because she was deadly serious in her reporting. I almost asked her what it mattered since I wasn't allowed to go outside anyway, but kept that to myself. I stretched and flopped back down on the pillows.

"I'll call when I'm ready for breakfast," I said, trying to tactfully get rid of her. There was no reason to jump out of bed. I had plenty of time to get dressed and discover the view from Ivan's balcony.

"Mr. Morozov wanted me to bring you to him as soon as you were ready," she said, wheeling in a rack full of my clothes. "I think he has something planned. He's been asking me if you were up yet every half hour since I arrived at six this morning but wouldn't let me wake you."

"Oh, okay," I said, perking up.

Plans? Maybe an outing? I didn't want to get my hopes up that things had really changed between us. After sleeping all night and most of the morning, I was beginning to wonder if I had dreamed the part where Ivan said he loved me. Once I got out of bed, I discovered I was ravenous, only eating a bowl of fruit since I was snatched.

Downstairs, Liz directed me to the formal dining room, but wrinkled her nose and said she'd be upstairs moving my things instead of joining me. I could see why she opted to stay away when I went into the grand, high-ceilinged room. The long mahogany table was covered with an array of guns. Tiny little pearl handled ones all the way to big, double barreled shotguns and ones that looked like they should only be seen in combat zones.

Ivan sat at the end of the table looking at his tablet and smiled up at me when I came in. He motioned to the breakfast laid out on the buffet, but I was more interested in the arsenal in front of me.

"You need to eat," he said, scowling.

To appease him, I grabbed a granola bar and munched on it while he explained the different types of weapons, then told me to choose one.

"Do you mean it?" I asked, almost choking on the dry raisin and nut bar. "You're going to teach me to shoot?"

"You said that was what you wanted, right?"

"I never thought you'd say yes." I threw myself at him and he hurriedly put down the semi-automatic rifle he had in his hands to catch me.

"A good first rule is to probably never fling yourself at someone holding a gun," he said with a laugh.

I wanted to get to shooting right away, but he insisted on showing me how to hold them, where the safety switches were, how to load and unload, and all the rules involved in order not to accidentally shoot myself or him.

"Don't ever aim at something you don't mean to hit," he said seriously.

I nodded, shockingly aroused by him as he speedily loaded up a smaller handgun for me to use. He put it in a case along with packing up a few others and told me it was finally time to actually pull some triggers.

"In the backyard?" I asked, wondering how the neighbors would take that.

He laughed and motioned for me to take my very own gun case. "Shooting in the backyard is a very good way to draw unwanted attention," he said mildly.

I had to stow my impatience for a little longer while he drove us to a private gun range out in the boonies. He walked ahead of me, beating back the overgrown palmettos that were trying to take over the path from the secluded driveway. The building was deserted, but Ivan had a key and let us in, flicking on overhead lights. It was quiet except for the hum of the fluorescent bulbs and Ivan told me to sit tight in the front area while he set up the range.

"No way," I said, following him.

He pulled me close and dropped a kiss on my head. "You don't have to be scared, but come along with me if you want."

Just then the sound of tires rolling through the gravel parking lot outside made him smile. "That will be Pavel. He runs this place for me. He'll set it up."

Pavel was a burly older man with a mouth full of chewing tobacco and a strange mix of Russian and redneck accent. He scratched his big belly as he greeted us, half joking and half grumbling as he went to get the shooting stalls ready for us.

Once it was ready, Ivan helped me get my ear protection on and slid the safety goggles over my nose, smiling at me as he watched me take my gun out of its case. I did everything he showed me and he deemed me ready to fire.

"It's about time," I said. He stood back and nodded for me to have at it and I unloaded at the paper target.

His mouth hung open when the gun was empty and I laughed at how exhilarating it was. He handed me one of his bigger guns while he reloaded mine and I quickly emptied that one as well. He reeled in my target and pointed out how I could get better accuracy. I was ready to keep practicing and eagerly held out my hands for my own little handgun back.

He shook his head and smiled at me. "You're certainly having more fun than I expected, my bloodthirsty queen."

"I'm not bloodthirsty." I put my hand over my stomach, never wanting to feel the helplessness that I had in the basement, not sure if I was going to live or die, or if my baby would ever have a chance to be born. "I only want to protect your heir."

He put my gun down and put his hand over mine. "Our heir," he corrected.

I believed him then that he loved me, that he didn't just keep me around for the baby. I desperately wanted to say it back to him, but the words caught in my throat. Wasn't I still his prisoner, love or no love between us?

"Will I be able to keep the gun in my room?" I asked.

He frowned. "Our room," he corrected again.

He was dodging my question and I changed the words, pressing my luck in testing him. "Can I keep it in our room, then? In the bedside table?" I never wanted to be without a means to protect myself again, but would he see my wanting the gun as a way to seek my freedom? Wasn't that really what I was angling for?

His jaw muscle twitched and he stared down at me silently for so long I was about to turn away to resume my practice. "Yes," he finally said.

"Yes?"

"You can keep it in the bedside table drawer. Whatever makes you feel safe." He looked down then, but I caught a flash of sadness. "I'm sorry I couldn't protect you, Reina."

The pain in his voice ripped right through me, making my hand move from my stomach up to my heart, that felt like it was being torn in two. "Ivan…" I wanted to tell him I loved him. I just needed—

A shot rang out from the front of the range, where we'd left Pavel sitting with his feet on the counter and a beer at his elbow. We both jumped and Ivan instinctively moved in front of me. It seemed unlikely to me that Pavel was shooting randomly and Ivan's face told me he didn't think so either. He grabbed me and hurriedly shoved me into a supply closet at the opposite end of the range, hissing for me to stay put before pressing my new gun into my hand. He shut the door, leaving me in darkness once again, and a much more cramped space.

Filled with confusion that threatened to turn to terror as I sat there clutching my gun, I decided to sneak out and see what was going on. I crept up to the door to the office and peeked around the slightly open edge. Sucking in a gasp, I ducked back out of sight, trying to process what I saw.

Poor Pavel was dead, the single shot had been for him, but it seemed like Ivan was the main target. A haggard, red-faced man had been holding his gun on Ivan. I crouched down below the man's eye level and looked again. Ivan's gun was on the ground and he stood tall and straight, staring down the man who'd gotten the drop on him.

"Why did you have to kill him?" the man raged, moving a step closer and shaking the gun at Ivan.

Ivan didn't move a muscle, answering calmly. "He took my wife. He broke our truce."

"Damn your truce. The fool only wanted a bit of revenge. He wouldn't have hurt her."

This had to be Anton's father, the head of Morozov's rival crime family. I begged to differ that his son wasn't going to hurt me. He'd taken me to a murder room right before Ivan showed up. Still, as he continued to rage at Ivan, I had to feel a little bit sorry for him. Not Anton, the old man who had the misfortune to raise him. I pressed my stomach with my free hand, then looked at the gun that I still held in the other.

This could be my chance to get away. I could sneak out and take Ivan's car, drive to the Keys and hop on a plane somewhere, anywhere but here. This was the shot at freedom I should have taken weeks ago, when Maksim was still alive, before my presence in Ivan's life kicked off this war.

I started to turn so I could crawl toward the back door, but then I saw the man's finger twitching on the trigger as he waved his gun at Ivan's face. My husband, the father of my baby, our heir. The man I loved. I knew I wouldn't leave him. Not couldn't, but wouldn't. As much as I belonged to him, he also belonged to me. Maybe I was bloodthirsty, who knew. But I wasn't going to leave Ivan and I wasn't going to lose him, either.

I stood up, raising my gun as I threw open the door. The man barely had a chance to glance my way when I aimed squarely at what I wanted to hit, and squeezed the trigger. The first bullet hit him in the chest and he fell backwards. I stepped forward, lowering my hand and shooting again to finish him off. I was Ivan's queen, after all, and wanted to be fit to reign by his side. I kept squeezing the trigger until Ivan slipped around behind me and grabbed my arm, gently lowering it to my side.

"It's empty, Reina," he said.

I loosened my grip and he took the gun, setting it on the floor at our feet. I stared down at the bullet-riddled body of the man who tried to steal my love away from me and turned to Ivan.

"We shouldn't have been here alone," I said harshly. "Pavel was useless. You should have had backup."

We couldn't even go to the beach without a team of men following him and he took us out to the middle of nowhere alone? I was furious at him, and wanted nothing more than to wrap my arms around him and kiss him senseless.

He took me into his arms and held me close, a harsh laugh rising from his chest. "I had all the backup I needed, my queen."

Chapter 20 - Ivan

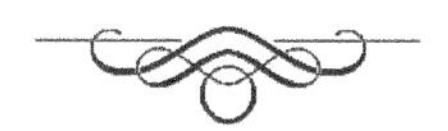

We managed to go two weeks without any new attacks and things seemed mostly calm. With the Balakin head and his son both out of the picture, his minions scattered and peace settled over Miami, at least for the moment. I was still staying close to home as much as I could, not wanting to be away from Reina for too long. When she wasn't with me, Dmitri followed her around at a distance, and her maid Hetty had finally returned to keep her company. I couldn't say things were perfect, or that Reina was completely happy, and it tormented me in quiet moments like now, when I had a lull in my work.

My phone dinged and I checked the messages, thrilled that I finally had some news that was sure to bring a smile to her face. I quickly called my contact.

"When?" I asked.

"Now," he answered. "I can start the video at any time."

"Do that. Send me the info so I can log in."

I ended the call and hurried to find Reina. She had taken to spending time in the kitchen, deciding she wanted to learn how to cook. She was there with our chef, rolling out pastry dough, and even though I knew she'd want to see what I was about to show her, I had to stop for a moment to take her in.

Her hands were covered in flour and her dark blonde hair was piled on top of her head and secured with a bright red bow, my favorite color on her. Her dark blue smock flowed over the swelling bump of our baby and she bit her lush lower lip as she looked down to read the recipe in front of her.

I loved her so much it took my breath away every time I caught her unaware like this. Even though she hadn't told me, I was sure she loved me, too. After all, she killed to save my life and she hadn't tried to leave me despite giving her almost as much freedom as she could want. Yes, she had to have guards, but she understood why now. I tapped at my phone to ready what I wanted to show her and when I looked up, she was smiling at me and wiping her hands on a dish towel.

I motioned for her to join me on the terrace and I led her to a shady spot. "Let's sit," I said. "I want you to see something."

We sat close together on a bench under a magnolia tree, the sound of one of the garden fountains gurgling behind a leafy hibiscus bush. I handed her my phone with the live stream already playing. Peering over her shoulder, the video showed a man half slumped in a chair, his face a mass of bruises. The man in charge of the questioning hauled back and knocked him almost playfully alongside his head.

Reina handed the phone back to me, a slight frown marring her brow. "This stuff doesn't freak me out anymore, and I'm really glad you're sharing your work with me these days, but you don't need to show me every single interrogation."

"Keep watching," I told her. "You'll want to see this one."

She took the phone and dutifully continued scrutinizing the scene. My man walked into the frame and leaned over the man in the chair. "State your crime," he said and moved back. "Tell our viewer why you're here."

The camera zoomed in on the criminal and he groaned, then seemed to accept it was probably better to get it over with. "I'm guilty of killing Jonathon Hall."

Reina sucked in a breath and her hands shook, but she held the phone closer. My interrogator asked the man why he did it.

"I was paid by a man named Phillip Lancaster, who wanted to buy his property. He gave me three thousand dollars."

Reina dropped the phone and doubled over. "That's all? That's all his life was worth?" She looked at me and her eyes were bleak. "Phillip was his friend. He was at his funeral. I thought he was doing me a favor when he offered to take the store off my hands." She made a retching sound and I patted her back.

"My men will have him in custody by the end of the day. We can turn him over to the police or take care of him like we're taking care of his gunman here."

Her hands tightened into fists and her breathing turned harsh. "He needs to suffer, really suffer. He's soft and he'll hate being in prison. Take him to the police," she said.

"And the man who pulled the trigger?"

"The same," she said. "I want justice, not revenge. That's what Dad would want." Her eyes narrowed. "But if there's any kind of loophole…"

I nodded. "I will follow them to the ends of the earth and make sure your father gets the justice he deserves."

My bloodthirsty queen's eyes sparkled up at me. "Good." She put her head in her hands, struggling not to cry. I wanted to let her know it was all right, she could feel however she needed to. That showing emotions didn't mean she wasn't strong. I couldn't have asked for a stronger woman.

"How did you solve it when the police couldn't?" she asked, inching closer to me.

I put my arms around her, trying to ease her grief. "The police have to abide by rules that I don't," I told her simply.

"You really do give me whatever I ask for," she said, sniffling.

"Always, Reina. If I can."

With trembling hands, she jerked off her rings and handed them to me, her lower lip jutting out. I was stunned and heartbroken, staring down at them. I couldn't find my voice to ask her why she'd taken them off or why she was rejecting me so suddenly.

"I want you to ask me to marry you again, for real this time." She gripped my shirt and pulled me close. "I love you, Ivan. I want to really be your wife."

I dropped off the bench onto one knee and held out the rings. "I'd happily propose to you every day of my life. Marry me. Be my queen, Reina."

She nodded, leaning over to kiss me, dragging my hand to her belly. "We're going to be a family," she said against my lips.

"Yes, now get these rings back on your finger where they belong."

"I only want the engagement ring until we have our real wedding," she said stubbornly.

I could have made her wear both rings. She was legally my wife after all. But this was what she wanted. I slid the big diamond onto her finger and kissed her palm before holding it over my heart.

"I don't want to wait long," I warned.

Her smile grew wider, her eyes hopeful. "If you let me invite my friend Lynn, we'll plan it in record time."

"Anything you want, my queen," I told her. "Spare no expense so we can show the world we belong to each other."

Chapter 21 - Reina

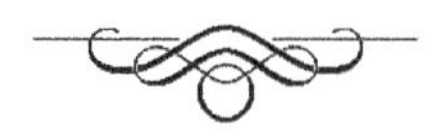

One month later

It was finally my wedding day. My real wedding day, one where I'd walk down the aisle with no threats held over my loved ones. In fact, Lynn was right beside me, needlessly fluffing up my massive ballgown skirt. She took all her vacation and sick days to be able to come down to help me plan, and she didn't know it yet, but Ivan was going to slip a pretty impressive check in her suitcase as thanks for being my Matron of honor. And she thought the gold earrings were such a great present I only wished I'd been there to see her face when she found it.

She mostly only knew about the nightclub, being one of Ivan's few completely legal businesses. There was no way I could tell her everything, and I barely told her anything, since she would never have been able to handle my new hardcore lifestyle. We still managed to talk almost nonstop while she was here, shopping for baby things and planning the wedding.

After she finished fussing with my dress, I pulled her close so we could compare baby bumps in the big, three way mirror in my newly remodeled dressing area. Lynn looked stunning in her mint green dress.

"I'm going to miss you so much after today," she said, tearing up.

"You're going to be in Miami another week," I said. The original plan was for Andrew to continue working and only come down for the wedding, but Ivan had thought that was too stingy and twisted their arms into accepting his South Beach apartment for a week's vacation after the wedding.

She snickered. "Yes, but you're going to be on your honeymoon and I'm going to be on the first vacation I've taken since Andrew and I were on ours. Basically, I don't think either one of us is going to have time to get together after today."

"Not until Christmas, anyway," I said. I was determined to keep my old friends, no matter how hectic my new life was. They were important to me, and thankfully, Ivan understood that and his generosity spilled over to them.

She gave me her present then, a sweet locket with a picture of her and Andrew on one side of the heart and my dad on the other. I blinked back tears so I wouldn't ruin my lashes and give Hetty a stroke having to reapply them.

"It's not corny?" Lynn asked.

"Not at all." I clasped the locket to my chest and then tucked it into my jewelry box. "He's finally getting justice," I said. We had just learned that my father's killer and the horrible, false friend who'd paid for the murder were both in custody without parole.

"They're sure to die in prison," she said.

I nodded, not at all worried about the outcome of their trials since Ivan promised justice, and he always kept his promises to me. "I think he'll finally be able to rest in peace."

We shared a silent moment, then she gripped my shoulders and looked at me seriously. "Are you really sure about this? I mean, it's all kind of sudden. You don't have to marry him just because you're pregnant."

I burst out laughing, but of course I couldn't tell her I was already married to Ivan and had been for months now. Lynn would never believe, let alone understand, everything we'd been through together to form our unbreakable bond.

"I'm sure," I told her.

"Okay." She hugged me, then fluffed my skirt some more. "I guess everyone with eyes can see how much he loves you."

"And I love him just as much."

Hetty hurried in with my bouquet, fresh bird of paradise and magnolias from our garden. "Everyone's ready whenever you are," she said.

I shooed her and Lynn ahead of me and as soon as they were out the door, I tucked my little gun in my garter. Ever since I took out Sergey Balakin, things were quiet and peaceful, but I wasn't going to take any chances on the happiest day of my life. Even with the discreet guards dressed as guests stationed everywhere and Ivan and his brothers sure to be packing, I just felt better with the cold steel against my thigh.

The wedding in our back garden was perfect. Thousands of twinkle lights, mountains of flowers, and a feast fit for the gods, my golden god included. No gun fights broke out, just a beautiful ceremony and a raucous reception afterwards. Each of Ivan's brothers jostled for a turn to dance with me, and I was delighted to be accepted so readily and treated like a true little sister. When I was dancing with Aleksei, a slow song started up, and Ivan jumped in between us, gruffly proclaiming they'd hogged me enough.

He took me in his arms and we swayed to the music under the lights and stars. I linked my hands behind his neck and pulled his head down for a lingering kiss.

"I love you," I said. "Did you know that?"

"I was hoping," he answered with a grin. His face grew serious and he tucked a strand of hair behind my ear. "You changed my life, my queen. I thought it was complete, but it was only when you danced into it that I learned what real happiness was."

My lashes couldn't withstand such a sweet speech and tears slid down my cheeks. He leaned over and kissed them away.

"I'll always be your queen," I promised.

A huge explosion sounded overhead and I jumped, whipping up my skirt to reach for my gun. Ivan laughed, pointing to the sky over the waterway. A brilliant shower of colors erupted above us.

"Fireworks, not fire power," he said, patting my skirt over my gun. "My sweet, bloodthirsty wife. I never need bodyguards when you're around."

I stood on my toes, gripping his shoulders. "You better not go anywhere without bodyguards," I warned. "Not even if I'm around. I can't bear to lose you."

He swept me off my feet and gave me a searing kiss that touched my soul. "You never will, my queen," he promised.

And he always kept his promises.

EPILOGUE - REINA

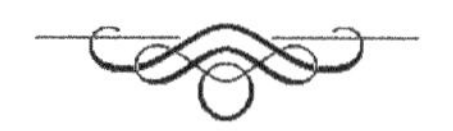

We stared into the bassinet, transfixed by our tiny, perfect daughter. Anya Diana Morozov, named after both of our mothers. She was only three months old and I couldn't imagine life without her. I was certain Ivan felt the same. He reached down and tucked his finger under her hand, smiling when her miniature fingers curled around his big one.

"You'll wake her," I said, reaching out to stroke her downy head.

"Don't you want her to be awake when my brothers get here? I want to show her off."

"Never wake a sleeping baby. And you showed her off yesterday when they were over."

"But isn't she different from yesterday? I swear she grows so fast." His brow furrowed and I thought he might cry.

I put my arm around him. "Big strong man," I teased.

"I'm weak where my girls are concerned," he said. He gently tugged his finger away and leaned back, sighing. "I can't take Nikolai and Aleksei today. Nikolai especially. He's been complaining nonstop about Grigory Lukin's visit."

"What did poor Grigory Lukin do to make Nikolai so mad?" I asked, always happy to catch up with my new family's problems. "And who is he again? Another cousin?"

"Not a cousin, but an old friend of my father's. He sent his daughter to study here when she was a teenager and she later became estranged from him." He shrugged. "I can't keep up with that, and to be honest, it's terrifying to think our princess might grow up to hate me."

"Never," I said, squeezing his arm. "You're already a perfect father."

He leaned to kiss me, smiling gratefully. He smelled good, fresh from a shower, and I scooted closer to him, sliding my hand in between the buttons of his shirt. He grinned. "Shall I cancel my brothers?"

"Can they deal with Grigory on their own?" I asked.

He groaned. "I wish I knew. I'm sure I'll hear more about it when they arrive. Something about an old contract with our father." He ran his fingers behind my neck and pulled me close for a kiss. "I'd rather spend this time that Anya's asleep with you, my queen."

Shivers of anticipation rolled up my spine at his suggestive look. Between the new baby and his busy schedule trying to juggle all his businesses, legal and otherwise, we didn't get that much time alone together lately. We both flatly refused a nanny, neither one of us being able to fully put our trust in anyone. Hetty watched Anya for an hour here and there but other than that, she was always with one of us.

I reached into his pants pocket and pulled out his phone, unlocking it with his code. We had no secrets from each other. I texted his brothers, telling them we'd reschedule for tomorrow instead, then tossed his phone onto the sofa beside us with a smile.

The baby stirred in her bassinet and we both held our breath. When it seemed like she would remain fast asleep, I climbed onto Ivan's lap, sighing contentedly when I settled on his thick bulge.

"Ah, my love," he said, his hands roaming up my back and dragging my shirt up with it.

I lifted my arms so he could take it all the way off and he leaned down to nuzzle my breasts, heavy and full still. My head dropped back as he sweetly cupped them, then ran his fingers down my sides, raising goosebumps. He was going to tease me? Well, two could play that game.

I writhed against his cock as I bent to kiss his neck, popping the buttons on his shirt until I could get my hands on his hard chest. We could be married for fifty years and I'd never be bored of him. My teasing was only making me suffer and I nipped at his earlobe as I continued to grind against him. He finally grabbed my hips and pulled me down hard against him.

"We haven't got much time," he said, his voice low and tempting. "Tell me what you want."

"I'll show you," I said, hopping up. I was wearing yoga pants so my striptease probably wasn't as hot as I would have liked, but his appreciative stare told me he was satisfied. I wriggled out of my clothes and hovered over him, taking his hand and guiding it between my thighs.

His fingers slid between my wet folds, already aching for his touch. As he caressed me, I undid his button and tugged down his zipper, catching his big cock when it bounced free. I watched his eyes run up and down my body as his fingers expertly worked my pussy. It would probably be months, maybe years before we could have long, leisurely sessions like we did before Anya was born, but he knew exactly how to bring me to ecstasy, even if we only had minutes.

With another glance at the bassinet, I climbed back on his lap, moving my hips with the rhythm of his fingers. He wrapped his free hand around my neck and pulled me close to claim my mouth, his tongue questing as his fingers pushed inside me.

"So close," I murmured, pulling away from his kiss to clamp my teeth onto his shoulder so I could muffle my cries. The second he tipped me over the edge I came down hard on his cock, unable to stifle my loud moan of pleasure.

He chuckled, his hands cupping my bottom as I rode him. "Do you think you can be quieter?" I gasped.

He shook his head, squeezing his eyes shut as I clenched around his shaft. He was mine and he needed to know it. He opened his eyes and gripped my hips to slow my frenzied movements.

"I'm not done with you yet," he said, voice full of wicked promise. Once again he found the swollen nub between my thighs, circling it until I panted for another release.

I thumped his shoulder, letting my head drop to touch his. "Please, Ivan," I begged.

My soft plea was all it took. He could never resist giving me what I asked for. With a roar that shook the windows, he pumped his seed inside me. I knew it was too soon, but I couldn't help wishing for a little brother or sister for Anya. With the perfect husband and father in Ivan, how could I not?

Fresh waves of pleasure washed over me and I let my voice join his. We both ended up laughing as I melted against him. For several long moments, we could only cling to each other and try to catch our breath.

"How is she still asleep?" I asked.

"Is she all right?"

We both hopped up, naked and sweaty, and peered at our tiny daughter. "She's fine," I whispered when I saw her chest rise and fall. I laughed. "We're ridiculous."

He gathered me in his arms and back onto the sofa, pulling a blanket around us. "Let's take a nap," he suggested.

It sounded deliciously decadent and I rested my head on his chest as he gently stroked my arm. "I don't even really need to ask you for what I want anymore," I said.

"Why's that, my queen?"

I smiled and closed my eyes, letting his steady heartbeat lull me to sleep. "Because you always just already know."

THE END

ABOUT LEXI ASHER

Lexi Asher gave up a promising career in the medical field to focus entirely on her family—and her writing. She lives in the beautiful, luscious Virginia countryside with her husband, 3 young children and 4 pets.

The Ashers' rustic cottage is bustling with activity all day long, so when Lexi wants to get her head down and let her creative juices flow, she will often take refuge in their beautifully ornate conservatory where Lexi does most of her writing.

When it comes to love, Lexi is a big believer in second chances—sometimes you just meet the right person at the wrong time. So, her stories often feature old flames that are reignited and broken hearts that are mended. But is love really better the second time around? Well, read and find out!

BOOKS BY LEXI ASHER

"Morozov Bratva" Series

The Russian Bratva of Miami has three rules: solve problems with violence, paint the streets with blood, and break hearts at will. They're not nice, they're not gentle, and they don't compromise. But behind closed doors, they'll show you what ruthless love really means.

Kidnapped by the Bratva

A Secret Baby by the Bratva

"Small Town Billionaires" Series

Pretend for the Billionaire

The Billionaire's Baby

The Billionaire's Next Door Neighbor

"The Crenshaw Billionaire Brothers" Series

Billionaire Brothers is where grumpiness and pain give way to romance and love. These loaded heirs may seem to have it all: money to burn, looks to die for, women to spoil. But it takes a special someone, a magical spark to reveal the real man behind the facade.

Grumpy Billionaire

Bossy Billionaire

Daddy Billionaire

"Lakeside Love" Series

Riverroad is a small town where everyone knows everyone, where the guy you've known since childhood turns into the hottest hunk around, where friends become lovers, and where everyday interactions between neighbors might just turn into steamy encounters when you least expect it...

Chasing A Second Chance

Chasing The Doctor Next Door

Chasing A Fake Wedding

Chasing The Cowboy

Printed in Great Britain
by Amazon

39832548R00071